THE INFINYDON

M.C. LORBIECKE

GOD SLAYER BOOK ONE

COPYRIGHT 2022

All rights reserved. This book or parts thereof may not be reproduced in any form, stored in any retrieval system, or transmitted in any form by any means—electronic, mechanical, photocopy, recording, or otherwise—without prior written permission of the publisher, except as provided by United States of America copyright law. For permission requests, write to the publisher.

This is a work of fiction. Names, characters, places, brands, media, and incidents are either the product of the author's imagination or are used fictitiously. Any resemblance to similarly named places or to persons living or deceased is unintentional.

This is a work of fiction. Names, characters, places, brands, media, and incidents are either the product of the author's imagination or are used fictitiously. Any resemblance to similarly named places or to persons living or deceased is unintentional.

Copyright© 2022 M.C. LORBIECKE

THE INFINYDON

M.C. LORBIECKE

Mother Nature takes revenge for man's exploitation of planet earth.

Dr. Evelyn Humbolt is a captivating professor who makes a startling discovery, a shapeshifting specimen that may just be immortal.

A primordial leviathan is resurrected and unleashed into the seas on a bloodthirsty mission to exterminate life.

A heretic is haunted by ominous prophecies; a fallen priest is torn by disturbing premonitions.

A diverse team of researchers is assembled to save mankind, but will they save humanity from extinction, or will the titanic infinydon trigger the end of life as we know it?

DEDICATION

First and foremost, I am dedicating this book to the love of my life and youngest child, for it was you who conceived this entire premise. As a family pastime, we enjoy discussing ideas and collaborating, cultivating them into complex plot lines. Anton, my quirky genius, hatched this idea and my husband, John Daniel, used his tenacity to chisel it into something viable. I took up the reins and breathed life into the leviathan, and, in cooperation, we wrought a primitive idea into a sophisticated storyline.
Secondly, I must thank my in-laws, John and Josie Lorbiecke, for it was you who literally fed us in those lean times while we fought our way through university so we could live and flourish in the future. You two are saints.
Furthermore, I would like to thank our extended family, who has cheered us on and cultivated us into the people we became: all my aunts and uncles, Longoria, Lyons, Lorbieckes, and Aguayos, the Stiths. All of my children, Anton, Emmie, Dominique, Sonya, and JJ, as well as Shawn and Adrian, Jacob, Charity, and Thaddeus. I also thank our doggy children for making us laugh when things felt too serious: Blade Lucius Lex, Cairo Black Wolf, Kira Little Mouse, and little Rukia. I wish to thank my author friends and family who paved the way for me and counseled me on my journey: Sandy Ogle, Noe Longoria, Jenny Bower, and Taylor Dawn.
As an educator, I must thank the two most wonderful teachers, Mrs. Alsup and Mrs. Johnson, for being ever

patient and kind. To all my students through the years who encouraged me in the classroom and kept me sharp as I taught fledgling minds.

I am also dedicating this legacy to those of our friends and family who have already passed: my mother, Lisa Longoria, Grandma and Grandpa Lorbiecke and Aguayo, Uncle Matt, Uncle JD, Aunt Diane, and Mike Lippert, and puppies passed: Brutus, Zoe, Mojo, Lady, Bugsy, and Killer.

There are not enough words to thank everyone who I would wish to mention, but if you have aided me and supported me on this journey, I thank you.

THE INFINYDON

M.C. LORBIECKE

CHAPTER ONE

BEGINNING OF THE END

A HEAVY-BODIED MOON hung on the horizon, obscured intermittently by clouds playfully teasing the watchman. Appearing later with summer constellations twinkling brightly above up, underneath nestled the earth, sea, and a sleepy vessel bobbing 100 miles off the coast. Tinges of light emerged from the east, threatening dawn. The salty spray misted Phan and his crewmates, who lived as if born of the sea.

Teetering on the deck's surface, his sea legs had lost agility thanks to the bourbon on his lips. The other whalers bedded down below deck hours ago. Resigned to resume his duty after tedious wandering, he returned to the crow's nest to watch for the Philippine Coast Guard. This entity could bring their illegal operation to an abrupt and unpleasant end. As he reached the top rung and mounted the platform, he stilled. He spotted what appeared to be an impossibly gargantuan fin through his drunken stupor.

Only half believing his eyes, he barked for the captain as he half-climbed, half-slipped down the ladder, making way for his fearless leader to scale the perch. The captain wasted no time responding to the panic in the young sailor's voice.

"Are they near?" the captain barked in Tagalog, peering through the darkness from the unlit craft. Fear the worst, he assumed that he'd been beckoned due by the policemen of the sea. Unable to decipher the sailor's babbling above the howl of the wind, he gave up. Squinting through darkness, he searched for the lights of an approaching vessel. When he failed to see any, he diverted his attention back to Phan, suddenly feeling foolish. Too many times, he had seen men experiencing imagined fear induced by a cocktail of sleep deprivation and exhaustion sprinkled with alcohol. It was not an easy life they led, but the substantial sum from a harvest of rare bounty was worth the risk of poaching the entire season. With his nervous tension ebbing, he couldn't help chuckling, warming with the feeling of having dodged a bullet. He felt as if their operation was nearly taken down, but then… wasn't! With an amused grin, he began to descend the ladder of his tiny observation deck when suddenly his ears were pricked by the familiar sound of breaching the water.

"Phan! Look Alive!" he commanded in delight at his good fortune. Never did a whale breach so near the ship. The sound of water displacement was huge. This one would fetch him an excellent purse. Having retaken his position up top, he skimmed the darkness seeking his target. He squinted into the night when he noted his man's failure to follow orders and spotted him crumpled up, holding onto the rail.

"Little Phan? Are you sick, Boy?" he heckled from his throne.

"Creature!" Phan shrieked in reply.

The captain's stomach tightened. Phan's voice was slick with terror, which did not indicate the silly ravings of a drunken man but the genuine feeling of a seasoned seaman who knew real danger when he saw it. The captain's grin faded. He began scanning the water more diligently. He slid down from his post and returned to the helm to relight the ship. Ablaze, he ran back out on the deck, heralding the rest of his crew. His blood turned to ice as he struggled to choke out orders for his men to attend. They all came running to the poop deck, a well-practiced assembly like clockwork. Pulling on hats and jackets, they emerged from below, prepared until they saw the beast that loomed only feet from the End of Days casting an ominous shadow as the sun surged over the horizon.

"Ready the harpoon!" the captain squawked. The men broke loose from shock and into action. Amazingly, like a colony of ants, they worked in unison to crane the heavy equipment, pulling levies and taking aim. Releasing, the spear whooshed, unswerving, at its target. The company fell silent as they waited, watching the rope whir past them, the crank turning as the ship's death dagger flew with interminable force. Their harpoon struck the animal's hide. They all stood in anticipation and watched in disbelief as it failed to penetrate her hide and fell away.

Appearing unphased, the beast sunk below the depths, leaving a vacuous trail of bubbles. Their craft bobbled dangerously. The crew stood motionless, bewildered, and uncertain about what might happen next. Silently they stood, every hair standing on end. Every nerve prickled intensely as if waiting for a bullet to leave the smoking barrel of a gun aimed directly into their paths. Finally, they began looking at each other as if to ask, did that just happen? A few quickly found the courage to peer into the water, discovering nothing. Phan was suddenly very sober. His eyes darted from his brothers in arms and to his captain…. questioning what that animal might have been.

    Without warning, a collision knocked them off of their feet. Everyone except Phan, who maintained his death grip on the railing. The behemoth broke the water so suddenly that it created a massive wave as she breached. Immediately, they all began screeching in fear. Pungent urine trickled down the pant leg of one man. Tear-streaked faces chanted prayers in hopes of redemption as the craft was lifted higher by the wave. They unanimously repented for their sins against nature and tearfully babbled hasty farewells.

The shortest man ran and sought cover below deck. Holding his breath, he gathered the gall to peek out the porthole. Darkness. He moved closer, fogging the window with his panicked exhalation. Blinking, he noticed the infantile sensation of soiling his pants, warm and sticky, pressing molding smoothly between his flesh and underwear. As the fog cleared, his eyes focused, and he saw the ribbing of a throat. The beast drifted backward. Teeth. She had several rows of teeth that seemed intelligently designed for grabbing, ripping, and tearing. Flexing her muscles, her jaw protruded beyond her broad snout in a horrifying display. She presented rows of gyrating scythes, sawing in opposing motions.

As she repelled further back, he noticed the pulsing of her monstrous gills moving her fins systematically. The monster moved so, maneuvering herself so delicately. Looking intently into the vessel, her large, catlike eye narrowed: searching. It was so fascinating that he forgot to be afraid, secure within the ship's safety. The tapetum lucidum of her mirror-like pupil flashed reflectively through the cabin. He ducked instinctively to avoid the searching flash of her eyeball, heart palpitating painfully. His eyes squeezed so tight that he saw spots. With his back to the wall, he told himself to calm down. In and out, he panted, his heart racing, one hand covering his eyes and the other clutching his chest. Sweat dripped from his brow. With intention, he began to relax. With one subaqueous explosion, his lungs were filled with water as the leviathan drove through the hold of the frigate and entered the cabin. Before he could react, his torso was severed cleanly from his trunk. Satisfied with the man's trunk held delicately within her jaws. She gave one vigorous flip of her keel and splintered the boat.

The men on the deck were flung into the air. The remains of their vessel tipped toward the horizon. Airborne, in slow motion, the men could see their foe in full view and gaze upon her prehistoric magnificence. Within a moment, the water turned crimson. Torn asunder were those who had made their fortune by turning the Asiatic waters red with the lifeblood of gentle whales. Their screams were drowned by tidal waves of powerful jaws, finding them individually with her dead-gray eyes, hunting with no remorse. During the struggle, their boat was broken up like a battered toy. This monstrosity and the vengeful sea seemed to work in harmony. In a few fleeting moments, they were done. One disembodied arm remained clinging to a piece of the hull.

Task concluded, she swam on, creating a mile-long wake with her powerful tail, poaching weapons disabled, appetite unabated by her meal. She swam on, still seeking. The only evidence of her encounter with this ill-fated crew was the blood-soaked harpoon which hung still attached to a piece of floating wreckage.

CHAPTER TWO

DOMINION

30 Days Earlier

THE EGYPTIAN COTTON of his hotel creased as Alexander Becker sat up, sleep interrupted by his phone. It hummed, signifying the CEO of Dominion Petroleum. The digital tune of Gran Vals sang out at 2:47, telling the Quality Control, Safety, and Environmental Manager that this was not a call to ignore. Never mind the miraculous quality of REM that he had been experiencing. A frantic voice buzzed on the other end of the line, confirming that this was no casual call.

"How bad is it?" Alex asked Tawny

Townsend as he rubbed the sleep from his eyes. As he stretched, bicep involuntarily flexing, he caught sight of himself in the gold-plated mirror on the far side of the room of the New York high-rise. Pensively rubbing at the stubble, the faint light of his phone illuminated his chiseled features. This suite was designated as his residence for the week as he brokered business out east. He responded mechanically, tuning back into the conversation as he roused more fully from his sleep.

"Of course." He paused, listening. "Yes. I'll compose a preliminary press release." he stretched, as she gave directive. "Yes. Wheels up in two hours? On my way." He ended the call and put his head in his hands, briefly regrouping in an attempt to digest the gravity of the devastation:

His mind was wrapped around what she had said: 300 dead, the rig a total loss; billions of dollars gone. How in the hell could this happen? Was his thought as he rose, lost in contemplation. His naked form entered the foyer of the restroom to shave and shower. Bathing quickly, only briefly allowing the hot water to pummel the sculpted muscles in his back and shoulders, now roused from sleep. Planted in front of the vanity, grooming, dressed from the waist down. He composed his thoughts subjectively, contriving a politically rational explanation for the press.

Alex entered the chilly New York air and quickly spotted the inky black car sent for him. It glided forward as he approached the curb. The Mercedes engine purred politely as he opened the door and instructed, "JFK."

"Yes, Sir." The driver pulled off, melting soundlessly into the burgeoning traffic. Alex pulled out his phone to make a call and then put it down.

"Good morning, Frederick." smiling wryly at his driver. It was unlike him to be so curt, let alone to such good help.

"Good morning to you, Sir." The driver said, tipping his hat slightly, making eye contact in the rear-view mirror for an instant before his eyes darted back to the traffic. He tapped the brakes to avoid hitting the vehicle that seized that split second of hesitation to dart out in front of him. "I thought you were in New York until Friday, but it's no matter. To the airport, we go." The driver chatted warmly, continually thankful to work with such a gracious and generous client. Alex patted the driver's shoulder in thanks, nodding in genuine apology, slid a philanthropic tip into the driver's hand, and then pulling out his phone made a video call.

"Townsend? Becker, here. I am en route." he reported keeping mental notes of the numbers. He listened intently as Ms. Townsend, the young, capable, surprisingly green CEO of Dominion Petroleum, rattled off the few facts she had been given, followed by well-thought-out directives. He took note of her composure on the video chat. She always impressed him. Also, she had really nice lips, plump. It was her azure eyes that always left a significant impression on him. What race was she? He wondered, noting the exotic slant of her eyes and freshly coiffed hair adorned by well-groomed face-framing brows. Alex was a little smitten with her, he realized. His mind wandered appreciatively, curious about what she looked like naked-faced, hair loose falling carelessly around her shoulders.

"It's the Mariana rig," she stated sharply with a thinly veiled bite in her voice, conveying unappreciation for his lack of attention.

"I know, it's bad." he inserted. "That many?" He hung his head. "I will." He said, nodding. "Headed there now. I'll be in the air within the hour. I'll keep you posted." He was the first to end the call, thinking to himself, how could this have happened? The geological survey revealed that it was a safe target for the most significant cache of oil in a long time. This reserve was supposed to catapult us to the top. Of course, not at the cost of lives, but those surveys determined that drilling there was safe. Well, relatively. The pressure of this explosion was so intense that nothing remained of the structure. No one had survived. He thought this devastation would be like none I had ever seen, trying to prepare himself.

"Sir," the driver interrupted. "We're nearing your destination. Five minutes."

"Thank you," Alex replied gratefully, readying his bags and himself for the next leg of his expedition.

CHAPTER THREE

THE PROFESSOR

DR. EVELYN HUMBOLDT was a petite spitfire of a woman. She had earned her doctorate degree against many odds. Although currently experiencing personal tumult, she was more fascinated and excited by her research subjects than ever before. Her thesis was an in-depth study of the evolution and adaptation of the order *Semaeostomae* and the family *Ulmaridae*: jellyfish. Evelyn was employed at California State University as a professor and researcher, working solo for the first time in her life.

When she was a sophomore in college,

she met a bold, beautiful, green-eyed rogue who was funny, had a remarkable intellect, and a vivid imagination. Adem Humboldt always kept her smiling with his sense of wonder, and once she got to know him, she desired nothing more than to be a part of his incredible world. Before they began graduate school, she became Mrs. Humboldt and Doctor a few years later.

Since then, the two had worked side-by-side on projects most often led by him until last spring, when tension in their marriage had reached a breaking point. One night, they had made the disastrous mistake of going to bed angry, and as the conflict escalated over the next week, he renounced science and decided to leave the department. A few days, Adem rented an apartment in the city to escape the warfare and ran away. Peace he sought: a space where he could write in solace and begin to explore his fascination with theology without criticism. As an accomplished double-major in science and religion and one of the most charismatic professors on campus, the university was more than accommodating when he expressed an interest in changing fields. With his new residence being closer to the school, he quickly immersed himself in budding collaborations and research with newfangled colleagues and became lost in distraction. She smoldered with jealousy and rage, unable to express her genuine opinion on his asinine behavior.

  Their marriage had been a fiery union of brilliant minds and amorous bodies. Sadly, fires that burn the brightest often don't burn eternally. They'd been together almost two decades. They'd had a good run. Their time had been primarily harmonious, but he seemed increasingly obstinate of late. These days, they could no longer seem to agree.

Even though they lived separately and were not in regular contact, they did share custody of a two-year-old malamute named Kanik. They met up every Sunday to hand off the dog. The truth was that both greatly anticipated their weekly meetings, each still deeply in love but both too stubborn to bend to the other's will. Evelyn was genuinely confused about where things went wrong even though the catalyst was glaringly evident to any objective lookers. It was complicated and muddy in her head.

It wasn't just one thing. Evelyn was

overcome with shame and anger from events in times past. She couldn't imagine how he could still love her despite all her own shortcomings. Ultimately, she feared that he might be better off with a new woman in his life. On his end, he was wrought by the guilt of his wrongdoings but refused to come to terms. The reality was that he could no longer see her love for him through the shroud of pain and sadness. He feared that holding a torch for her might be pointless after all this time but couldn't bring himself to let her go. The idea of his life without her didn't seem like anything but a dark and lonely place. To him, she was his world.

For these reasons, they stubbornly waited for the other. Quietly, each waiting for their partner to submit, crack, express hope, or take any step so this whole horrific break could end and safely fall into each other's arms. Each weekend for the last few months, she had behaved coldly, and he had just been a jerk, both too prideful and afraid to honestly admit their feelings in the hope of reunification.

This Friday afternoon, Evelyn was on autopilot in the lab, consumed by her anxiety about their upcoming visit. She was considering cutting her hair the next day to see if he might notice.

If Adem did, would he say anything? Would he like it? Would he hate it? she wondered. She couldn't imagine that he would say anything no matter how it looked. Her pulse began to quicken as this internal dialogue escalated in her head. Shaking her head at the ludicrous nature, she pushed the hypothetical dilemma out of her mind laughing aloud at herself for getting offended over something that had yet to occur. Anyway, she enjoyed having long hair. So, there would be no point in cutting it now. If he didn't want her anymore, she reasoned that changing her hair wouldn't change his heart.

Evelyn ordered herself to stop obsessing over him and pay attention to these extraordinary little gems. Redirected her thoughts to her new research subjects: "immortal jellyfish," as the media called them. Turritopsis dohrnii, their scientific name, was what she called them. The doctor was curious about how these remarkable creatures had remained undiscovered for so long. Then again, the ocean is vast, and so much is yet to be discovered.

Contemplating these ramifications, someone buzzed, asking to be let in at the glass doors to the lab. Met with a goofy grin, she snickered. Hank was here! Hank was a tall, lanky, well-muscled student whose body and mind were maturing into manhood handsomely. She anticipated that he'd be a beautiful mess by thirty that any woman would be lucky to catch. He was a bright but melancholy science major with exceptional musical talent. Admirably, he was willing to work and work hard, which the doc loved best of all. She greeted him warmly and told him to glove up to take some fecal samples from the nursery tanks.

"*Shit!* My favorite!" he responded with fictitious morose. He pulled his glossy hair up into a knot. Surprised by his attitude, she turned around to see him grinning at her.

"Yes, Dear. I knew it was, so I saved the task all for you! Come on, though. You have to admit that these are some pretty fascinating feces!" with a playful expression, she did a little spin and a funny tap dance, trying to sell him on her perspective with the aid of some humor. She ended the number with the tip of an imaginary top hat and some dazzling jazz hands.

"Yep!" He said in good-humored defeat, raising his eyebrows at her, snapping the gloves on his wrists as he always did. She was cute, he thought warmly. He admired her, and she never gave him the real shit work like mopping. Working here was pretty good for him. With a disarming smile, he examined each specimen with focus and proficiency, recording his findings as he went. Evelyn watched him nodding to the rhythm of whatever caterwauling was being birthed out of the end of his earbuds, one implanted in his ear canal, the other dangling so he could still listen if need be.

Evelyn finished her inventory and followed behind her assistant, gathering the dirty slides and beakers that needed washing. She bypassed the procedure of putting them on a tray. It was just a few things and turned to head to the sink. Struck by the urge to ask him if he had seen the hilarious picture, she had hung up of him on the bulletin board in the common area, knowing that this realization would make him cringe, she turned. The toe of her shoe caught on the centrifuge cord, and down she went, glass in a shatter. The wind knocked out of her out momentarily. She rolled over onto her back, catching her breath when she noticed a rather deep gash on her palm and tried to sit up.

"Jeeze! What the hell?" which was Hank's way of asking what happened. He knelt over her and the broken glass, quickly becoming an impressively bloody mess. "Easy, Doc. Just rest a sec," he coddled.

"Oh! *That* cord, is what!" she explained, realizing that she was to blame, knowing that all loose cords should be taped to the floor. She shooed him away. "I'm fine," she promised. Despite her protest, he helped her up and hovered nearby as she walked carefully to the sink, leaving a bloody trail along her path. She put her hand under running water, and Hank saw that, though deep, it was a relatively small cut and that it would probably be more helpful for him to clean up the mess than to keep pestering her. Grumbling, she held her hand under the running water and spotted a tiny shard sticking out of the wound. She grabbed a pair of tweezers and pulled it out, lecturing him on safety precautions in a lab, explaining that this could have been worse. She had seen a nasty lab accident, she preached.

"Even though all these rules seem nit-picky, they have all been written for good reason. Scientists don't make pointless rules. They need to be followed if you plan to work in a laboratory. It's black and white: uncomplicated." she trailed off, now more to herself than to him, wincing as she squeezed the cut, examining the wound for debris. She quieted as she looked into the open laceration, closely assessing the damage. She decided butterfly bandages would fix this, not wanting her mistake to become university knowledge.

"Yep," he said, filling up the mop bucket. Pulling out the other earbud in case she said something of actual importance. "Should really follow the rules, Doc," he agreed. "You sure you're, okay?" When she didn't answer, he said to himself, "I like this song." And reinserted one bud. Then to her... or himself, he said, "Hey, I like this song called 'Pianos Become the Teeth.' I think I want to get that tattooed on me, maybe on my butt, with like a yellow flower or something. That would be gangster. Probably the right cheek, not the left."

"You could," she envisioned. "Marigolds are very gangster! But how many people would see a tattoo on your rear end?" she asked quizzically and with amusement.

"Lots of people!" he proclaimed with conviction. "I'm in a band!" he reminded her with clarification.

They laughed. Feeling a little woozy, she was thankful that he was here. Her assistant brought the first aid kit and a stool. He put the cleaning supplies away and sat next to her watching her disinfect and wrap her hand. Observing her, he shared his plans for the weekend.

"Saturday, my band has a gig in Long Beach. That venue has the best fish tacos. I've never played there, but I went before when my boy Marco played there. We said I was his boyfriend, and they let me in for free." His eyes beamed with the sweet memories of him and his friends out on the town. "Instead of money, they paid in tacos which were so worth it. I ate fifteen tacos because he hates fish, and they were just there. Plus, my ex had just broken up with her man. So, you know. You never know!" he said, grinning.

"You lost me!" she proclaimed.

"Her best friend told my little brother that she was thinking of seeing me there. So, I mean…. you know!" he explained eloquently.

"Okay. Yes. I think I know." she chuckled, almost envying his carefree youth. Then again, not. Although this beautiful young man had a world of glittering unknown possibilities in front of him and an uphill climb of finding himself to do. She had a bright future all figured out; she just needed to seize it. She had everything she wanted except for one thing.

Hmmm…. If only Adem would make a move. One of the things she admired about her husband was his obstinate nature. As Evelyn and Hank followed the procedure to close the lab for the week, she leaned over the giant aquarium to admire her precious specimens, Hank crouching down to get a lateral view.

"Look at that one." she puzzled. "It seems like it's grown significantly in just a day or two."

"Which one?" he asked.

"That one. The bigger one!" she said, pointing clearly from the top. A fat droplet of blood rolled from her palm, down her fingertip, and into the water. They watched as the animal that came into contact with the globule morphed immediately, displaying six to eight tiny serpentine appendages with jaws. Violently, they breached the surface of the water in response. As the crimson stimuli dissipated, they watched the creature morph back into seemingly aimless shapes. They turned and locked eyes as if to ask for clarity or at least some kind of confirmation.

"What the fuck?" Hank spoke first. "What was that?" he raved. Not having an answer or point of scientific reference, she sat at a loss for an explanation for what they had just witnessed!

"Do it again!" he suggested in excitement.

"Yes." She acknowledged logically. He pulled out his phone and removed both earbuds, which indicated that she had his full attention. There is no higher-level display of attention from Hank than no earbuds.

"I'm recording! Go!" he encouraged. At his prompting, she moved to touch her thumb to her pinky, causing another droplet to travel down her palm, her middle finger, and then roll down, down, down. She suddenly closed her fist, stopping the flow.

"No." she hesitated. "This isn't a proper setting for advanced experimentation. "I mean, first, we need to collect preliminary data. We need a control group. We must establish a baseline first, or our findings may not be legitimate. I mean, they could be argued. They could be disproved. They may not even be reproducible." At this, Hank stood, put his hands on her shoulders, leaned down so they were face-to-face, and instructed her.

"We have two tanks. One psycho fish;

one regular. There's your control group and your experimental group. Do it."

"They're not fish," she mumbled, considering his reasoning and found it somewhat sound. "Yes!" She agreed overall. "Get me a stool! I'm scared! What if it bites me?" They talked excitedly as he retrieved a step stool. She climbed the two rungs with his hand steadying her. "Ready?" she asked, prompting him to record. He nodded. He stood back and splayed his feet as if preparing to take the recording of a lifetime. She looked at him. "No." she shook her head with resolve.

"Yes!" he determined.

"Okay!" she agreed. She looked to confirm he was ready.

"Go." he directed impatiently.

She squeezed her hand, and they

watched breathlessly as the rotund droplet of blood rolled and hit the water. Nothing happened. Bewildered, they both sat watching nothing out of the ordinary occurring. The animals undulated and swam about just as harmlessly as they typically did.

"Do it right on top of one of them. Maybe aim for the big one again," he suggested, still filming. Nonplussed, she began to follow his instructions. She turned her torso to position her hand over the biggest, no, the smallest one, she decided out of great curiosity. She paused.

"Are you sure we should?"

"Do it!" he cut her off. She squeezed her hand, and two droplets fell, making the three closest specimens lurch and morph, nearly cannibalizing each other until the blood dissipated. They quickly reassumed a gelatinous form that floated aimlessly, as gently as lilies on the water. The scientist looked at her young apprentice, astonished. He was now recording her and her face.

"Doc?" he asked as she stared blankly. "Did we invent something?"

"Invent? No, but discover? Yes! Something huge! Holy moly! Holy moly!" she exclaimed, hurriedly climbing down from the stool with one hand. Stealing her off of the last step, picking her up, he hugged her excitedly. They danced around and talked enthusiastically until they saw four people outside the testing center looking in to see what was happening.

"Shhhh...." she chortled. "We should settle down. I mean, this is big! This research will be taken away from me and given to someone higher up on the food chain if this isn't handled with kid gloves; this project is mine. Hank! This is important. Don't tell anyone. Don't share that video with anyone! Except me! Send that to me immediately!"

"Got it! No one! I mean, I already posted it to Snap, but I only have like 25 friends on there, and they're all dumb. Well, kind of dumb. I mean," he searched, "They don't look at my streaks anyway! It's no big deal." he assured her confidently. She stared at him dumbfounded. "Yeah. Okay. I'll take it down."

"Thank you. So, now what do I do? I can't trust this with anyone? Who do I talk to? This is groundbreaking!"

"Dr. A.," he replied densely, as in Dr. Adem Humboldt, which Hank had grown accustomed to calling him since there were previously two Dr. Humboldts in the lab.

"What? My Adem? Oh, no. I can't. Besides, he's no longer a scientist."

"Ummm... "I know you're all lovesick and all that, but you can. Also, he's, like, the smartest guy in the universe except you, and he is still a scientist even if he's making out with the Bible right now. He cares about this stuff and you, and then... maybe you two can-"raising his eyebrows in unison. "Huh?" he smiled. Perplexed, she glanced down at his hands and saw him perform some libidinous actions between his right and left fingers. She slapped his hands down, grimacing.

"Weirdo!" she responded in embarrassment.

"Just call him," he said, sighing as he

unlocked his phone a read a message from his TikTok account. "Well, my ride's here. Yeah, are you sure you're, okay? I've gotta go."

"Yes. I am fine! Thank you very much, young scholar," she said, smiling, overwhelmed by her affection for this young man. "Goodnight," she said. He slung his bag over his shoulder and let himself out. She headed toward her office to sit in preponderance. She turned back when she heard the door slide closed. "Good work today," she hollered after him.

Waving without looking back, just as nonchalantly as he did any other day, both earbuds inserted, probably listening to 'Children with Teeth' or whatever that band was called. Having ensured the door was locked, the woman was suddenly overwhelmed with the feeling that she had a priceless treasure that needed intense guarding. She shut her office door, turned the light out, and sank into her chair as she often did when alone. Her marine aquarium cast a verdant glow over the office. Decompressing, she listened to the bubbling water. Alone, she contemplated what she had just witnessed, questioning her perception. When her eyes refocused, she noticed an uncanny resemblance to images on the dust-jacket of her old mythology and political science books on her long-neglected bookshelf. Her expression brightened with exhilaration, confusion, and disbelief. She picked up the hard copy of Leviathan or The Matter, Forme and Power of a Common-Wealth Ecclesiastical and Civil written by Thomas Hobbes, initially published in 1651. Hers was an authentic print from 1909. According to the prologue, the fiend illustrated was described as a beast washed ashore after a typhoon. Looking at that ancient image, she had an inconceivable epiphany.

CHAPTER FOUR

SPECTER

DELSIN BUCK WOKE with a start, dark eyes blinking, jolted awake by the screeching brakes of the morning train. From his camp near the tracks, he felt more in touch with nature than any of the dark passageways he'd slept in the last year. The young man considered his gray tent sheltered by these proud trees a decent make-shift home, at least for now. Living in Broken Arrow, Oklahoma, near the tracks wasn't ideal, but he enjoyed the elder groves of cypress, dogwood, and elm in this area. The ample vegetation provided shade from the sun and shelter from the night winds. It was peaceful here. He could hear birds in the morning and smell the rushing water from Arcadia Lake, but this spot was lacking one thing: nourishment. He kicked his way out of his Coleman Autumn Trails sleeping bag, skin damp with perspiration. This blessed sack had provided sweet relief last winter, but it had turned into a sweatbox since the bloom of spring. Delson asked himself why he didn't just sleep on top the bag to cushion himself from the iron ground. He didn't know why but he liked the security of being wrapped up tight inside, he reasoned. Wrestling the tongue out of his right boot, pulling the leather on but not bothering to tether the laces, he was ready.

A smart man would go into the city and find a sheet to sleep under so you can lay on the sleeping bag, his conscious badgered. *Stupid*, his internal monologue accused, *but first breakfast and drink*, his mind reasoned. Definitely drink, he thought in desperation. Every day, he woke parched, his eyes bloodshot from the previous day's consumption. Del picked up a mostly empty water bottle and grimaced as the tepid, stale fluid failed to slake his thirst. While that liquid eased the tightness of his desiccated throat, it was not what he truly desired. Vodka was his drink of choice, his medicine, to quiet the many voices in his head.

Delsin was a twenty-one-year-old Cree native. He was considered a "kithla," or someone who knows things in the community where he was born and raised. Members of the Cherokee tribe thought these people to be prophets who could converse with the Great Spirit. Unfortunately, the Great Spirit was not very happy with his people or the earth's inhabitants of this day and age. The actions of mankind and the current state of our world was considered a cacophony of sins.

Many days, Delsin peddled glimpses of his visions for cash at the intersection of Kenosha and First. He used to repress them and try to keep his revelations to himself, but in the last year or so, they had begun to roar, and the only way he could keep his sanity was to express them to anyone who would listen. Del had always been hardworking. He had worked at the store on the res for many years, which kept his mom and sister fed. Recently, the spirits seemed to have taken up permanent residence in his head. He could no longer work or live his life among his people.

Shamefaced, he had left home and gone

on the road, drinking heavily to dull the noise. He had even been institutionalized earlier this year when he was found in a bad state in Oklahoma City. When the police tackled and arrested him, he had multiple self-inflicted wounds on his forehead and temples from smashing his head into the wall of some alley. The hospitalization had brought him true relief because the prescribed medications evoked a mental fog and blackout better than any booze. During his 48-hour intake, the physician on-call decided that Del was suffering from Schizoid Personality Disorder and drugged him heavily due to the severity of his episode. Unfortunately, the physician that relieved her on Monday decided that this handsome, smooth-tongued patient was a drug seeker and discharged him hastily without any aftercare.

Since then, he'd been chasing that state of bliss that only the specter named Risperidone could bring.

Having rinsed the night's sweat away at his meager water reservoir, he donned a flannel over his yellowing undershirt. Unable to conceal his thick build, ragged jeans snugly hugged his formidable frame and size thirteen boots with the frayed laces that slapped the ground as he ventured forth. Clothed and somewhat washed, he began the trek to his daily haunt. He had a dingy coffee can in hand with "Change for Change" scrawled onto it in white acrylic. As the voices began to chatter, he pursed his lips and shook his head, begging for quiet as his almond eyes stared into oblivion, grappling with dark prophecies of the end.

Stationed at his post, he sat cross-legged, leaned back into the stop sign, and permitted the fog of the ancestral guides to fill his mind. When the clouds began to settle, Delson began to vocalize what came to the forefront of his consciousness.

"Hi-ye-gi! Wake up, my brothers and sisters. Our world," he paused, seeming to be observing something in another world, "Our world is crying! When white invaders first came to our land, ambassadors of the Great Spirit were sent to guide them through the land and beg for peace in the countryside. 'You may harvest, but you must not rape. You may hunt, but do not murder,' they were told. Like my warrior ancestor, Kennekuk of the Kickapoo tribe said, 'My father, the Great Spirit, has placed us all on this earth; he has given our nation a piece of land. Why do you want to take it away and give us so much trouble?' He learned through death and resurrection that regardless of race or religion, peace and prayer with divine guidance is only the way to live. Use your Christian church alter and your One True God or use ancient prayer sticks, the spirit world, and the ancient creator to seek truth, but we must preserve our paradise, our earth, or damnation will come soon. We must repent and show temperance, for she is coming. I see her approaching our shores. My elders have often foretold crises in the past: Small Pox, the Long Walk, and now a new virus. We must stand and renounce our greed and do the ghost dance again. We must call on the favor of our spirit guides and grieve now for the pretty princess. She and her people have been lost and can never be recovered. She will not fall alone, my brothers and sister. We shall all turn to ash together!"

His wailing began to taper as the visions dissipated, and he began to rouse back to consciousness. Suddenly self-aware and a little embarrassed at his state, he felt his throat closed as anxious tears dashed down his cheeks. Delson collapsed from a stiff sitting position down onto his elbows on the sidewalk. Blinking, he wiped his tear-streaked face with a dirty sleeve. He looked down to see his coffee can filled with a five-dollar bill, several ones, and some spare change. There was a cold cup of coffee at his feet that some kind passerby had left some time ago. He took a deep, ragged breath trying to slow his pounding heart. As he uncurled his body from the position of his trance, he noticed a boy of about eleven recording him on an iPhone from a third-floor apartment balcony. Fearful of the lunatic, the kid ducked back into the third-story window, snickering. The kid wasted no time uploading the video to Donut Diggler Kid's YouTube account, where his one hundred fourteen subscribers were anxiously awaiting some juicy new hilarity. Diggler Kid uploaded without editing and began to peruse YouTube for any jewels published in the last hour since he'd logged off. While on YouTube, he passed by the Dateline video about the unexplained disappearance of the Bonnie Baroness's cruise liner to binge on clips of footballers and gym rats farting at inopportune times.

    Delsin was rigid from sitting on the

pavement for who knows how long. He lost track of time in those states. Slowly, he rose, stretching. According to the shadows on the sidewalk, it was at least midday. He picked up the small cup of coffee and drank it in a few hearty gulps. It was stagnant, cold, and bitter. He shivered and gave thanks for the offering. He envisioned it was left by a woman with a small dog, afraid but hopeful for the poor man on the street, but who knows. I could have been anyone. That was more of a notion than a prophetic vision like those that so vividly overtook him.

Feeling encouraged by these tokens, yet discouraged and bitter, he decided to get a bite to eat and a pint of Imperial vodka. That should hit just hard enough to let him fall asleep without a hangover. Clarity was necessary for the following day when he had his visions. He just needed temporary respite from the clamor, not total silence. Dejected, he felt that his attention to his visions was more critical than ever. Time was of the essence. Somehow, he just knew.

CHAPTER FIVE

TASMANIAN TIGERS

DOCTOR EMMIE LONGORIA heard a rumor, a delicious rumor, that on the mainland of Australia, there were sightings of Tasmanian Tigers: *Thylacinus cynocephalus*. There have been over 7000 documented sightings. An animal that has been deemed by the scientific community to have gone extinct nearly 100 years ago. Previously abundant, this animal was hunted mercilessly. Furthermore, their well-being was jeopardized due to habitat loss thanks to man's encroachment. Once the countryside became an agricultural region and thylacine fed on livestock for survival, farmers went on a mission to eradicate them. In the 1930s, the animal believed to be the last was captured and housed as a captive until its death.

Emmie was following an extension of her Ph. D. studies as a media research journalist minoring in the biological studies of obscure and extinct species. This distinguished young lady was investigating the existence of a thylacine doe who'd been reported with a pair of joeys. There was a river basin where the trio had been caught on trail cams by the Department of Primary Industries, Water and Environment. Emmie believed them to be living in the area. She just needed definitive proof to put them back on the CITES list, Convention on International Trade in Endangered Species of Wild Fauna and Flora, to ensure their protection.

She had been granted review of the footage of *dingos* gnawing the head off of kangaroo carrion under cover of night. Seeing the doe's joeys hop and pounce in a way which was not mechanically canine, spotting their short ears and elongated alligator-like jaws, slender bodies ending in thick tails, all told her these were a female thylacine with her young. Only after she brightened the footage digitally could she see a faint outline of seventeen telltale tiger stripes on the doe.

This footage prompted her trip to the outback, where she planned to camp out with her Nikon D850 DSLR Camera. Abandoning her Subaru back at her campsite, she lugged her drape, a mat, a pack with snacks and water, and a tripod downhill. Emmie intended to set up a fort in a thicket with canvas tented all around, sitting all night for a series of weeks, photographing the nocturnal wildlife until she eyed her target. Slapping at the insect threatening to fly right up her right nostril, she spied the area she would set up. Finding the perfect copse of trees near the river yet uphill enough to give her a clear vantage, she quietly put out her gear. Beaming at the complex chorus of the night announcing the setting sun: calls of birds aplenty, wedebills and their kin warbling, wild cockatoos crying, amphibians crooning harmonizing with the sounds of mammals who'd slept through the heat beginning to rouse.

Camp established; Emmie found a comfortable position in view of the rushing water through a large peephole in her bivouac.

Quietly, she loosed her canteen from the thong on her backpack, remaining silent to avoid exposure to the animating wildlife. Being conservative, she took a few deep cool pulls from the metallic portal, comforted by the titanium aftertaste that lingered when she drank from this old faithful vessel. This bottle was her father's, who carried it with him in the war. He was a tough man, brutish according to some, but he was a gentle giant and deeply intellectual too. Nourishment from this flagon felt as close to a hug from her father's mighty arms as she could get alone in the bush. This man pushed her to pursue her dreams no matter the cost. She finally arrived at her dream destination through blood, sweat, and poverty. Graduated, her studies were now funded by the Wonambi Conservatory

Coalition, a group of prosperous preservationists who hire researchers and zoologists to investigate and study wildlife, specifically endangered Australian and even a few recently classified extinct. With all her travel expenses covered and a substantial weekly stipend, she could focus on her work. When she was burdened with starvation and anxiety that plagued her concentration while researching for her graduate work.

With the umber of evening radiating a carmine cast over the landscape, the cicadas began their ballad of the bush, heralding the warm evening as summer night tide fell. Laying back on her pack roll, knowing that she would hear rustling should larger animals approach. She listened. Em gazed at the twinkling stars wink at her from the heavens.

Breathing deeply, she inhaled a perfume of eucalypti and river water. She heard a rustling at the edge of her blind. She sat up to attention, knowing she could encounter venom. Emmie was delighted when a common scaly-foot legless lizard slithered up and over her bag and out of the other side of her hide, paying her no heed. *Pygopus lepidopodus*, she mused. Did you evolve from, or are you evolving into a serpent? she wondered. She was drawn out of thought when she heard the drumming wing beat of some sparrows. She peeked out of her peephole to watch a flock dancing and playing on the rocks at the water's edge, dipping their toes and beaks in a while, cheeping a merry tune. They were quickly joined by a starling mimicking their song, which soon began his own lively whistling tune: *Sturnus vulgaris*,

Emmie recalled. She took out her audio recorder to start recording a session. With the wheels of her recorder rolling, she adjusted the knobs in time to catch the funny song of a far-off Kookaburra.

Now that dusk had fallen, she began to watch through her camera lens and saw thorny lizards, some impressive beetles, and a quiet mob of kangaroos over three hours. Before returning to their respective camps, they all came to the water to drink and cool off. It wasn't until the moon had traveled across the heavens and had become shrouded by the northern mountain range that she was overcome by fatigue. The amalgamation of a lack of wildlife activity combined with the passivity required by a photographer in hiding, she resigned herself to taking a fifteen-minute nap. Setting her watch to vibrate when the small hand reached the four, she settled her head back on her backpack, reaching up she moving her long thick braid from underneath her. She spread her button-up flannel over her goose-pimpled arms like a throw blanket to reduce the naked feeling of sleeping outside in the outback.

She felt insignificant in the open with the stars staring down at her. What a big giant world this is, she reflected. She had just begun to doze when she thought she heard large soft feet padding as if in a trot, halting, unsure. She laid still, holding her breath, and squinted her eyes into the darkness as if that would sharpen her hearing. Not able to hear much over the subtle chirp-hum orchestra of Gryllotalpa's cricket song in the grass, she let out her breath, ribs expanding neath her hands. Maybe she had dreamt the experience, she considered. Letting her eyes flutter closed again, knowing her respite was nearly spent, she hearkened. Taking a deep belly breath, she smiled, realizing, whether this academic found what she sought or not, there was nowhere else she'd rather -

 Her thought cut short when she heard a yip and then a strange growl. The hairs that had just lain down in repose stood up to alert. Body stiffened. She desperately wanted to look out of the peephole but reached up, hit record on her camera, and laid still to the happenings. Afraid that if she sat up and jostled around, she would spook the animals that she just knew were thylacine. Emmie heard padded footsteps break the surface of the water and smaller bodies splashing carelessly, a mother wolf's grunt seeming to shush them. The joeys quieted and swam quietly. She could hear the water sloshing as they sounded to get in and out. Finally, she heard a scuffle accompanied by the playful sounds of wet paws and the purring of the doe from the water. With this bit of commotion, she decided to sit up and spy. She clenched her abs, trying to rise without disturbing the fabric of her hide. It was so dark that she suddenly saw white splotches as her pulse raced in excitement.

Upright, she closed her left eye, peeping. There before her was a two-and-a-half-foot tall Tasmanian Tiger and her three joeys. Her striated back shimmered, droplets of river rolling off her coat. Gracefully she abandoned the water and, belly full of water, rounded up her young to return home. Repressing the urge to clap her hands enthusiastically, she clenched her fingers, biting her knuckle. Checking the lens to ensure she was capturing them; she saw that she was pointed too far right and turned the rig which made the tiniest squeak. Pricking at this sound, Mother stood on her hind legs glaring into the darkness. Wiggling her nose, she cataloged the alien scent detected. Mother perused her database of odors and decided that this one envisioned danger. With authority, she stomped her front foot, making a surprising sound, a hissing sound bringing her ruffians to attention. They took notice, looking at her for direction. She suddenly bounded away from the water and broke into a gallop. The three joeys followed tightly behind her. Emmie sat awestruck, silent, pulse pounding in her ears. She wanted to shout it to the rooftops. Fortunately for her, she didn't have to as a roost of flying foxes began to screech beyond the clearing over an apparent disagreement as the sun started to paint the horizon pink with the brilliant promise of a new day.

CHAPTER SIX

BLACK LOTUS

ANTON ISAAC CLOSED his browser windows, clicked initiating his ritual data-wipe, and shut down his Alienware laptop. Squinting, he pushed his glasses up onto his nose and gave a covert wave to the Black Lotus Coffee Shop staff. He shouldered his messenger bag, snatched up his keys, and turned to take his leave. There was a suspect newcomer in the shop today. Anton's programming had detected a breach, not just any violation, but from an invader within a twenty-foot radius. Government Sucker! He thought to himself, sending a seedy bot back the hacker's way that would infect her computer and everyone on her network. He'd be halfway to Palm Springs before she caught wind of his antics and threw out her coagulated coffee in frustration. He loved the game, and he played it well.

Anton didn't have a traditional job. Much to his mother's chagrin, he had amassed significant wealth by writing code for Bitcoin at the tender age of eleven. Anton took that as his cue to party when his parents told him to take his bath and go to bed. Starting at a tender young age, he spent nights surfing and hacking from the pink glitter Nintendo DS that his sister discarded. By age ten, he had already been banned from technology at school and home because his parents had noticed a strong proclivity that made everything else in his life seem insignificant. He became obsessed, which gave them great concern. Being on the spectrum, they sheltered him and worried about his self-regulating ability. That was ten years in the past now. More amazingly than how he gained his fortune was how, when he was eleven, he lost over 2.3 million dollars. It was stored on a Transformer jump drive that his blind and deaf chihuahua ate thanks to a misplaced glob of peanut butter. That particular day, he was tardy in serving her a second lunch thanks to a late school bus. When he found it some days later, he didn't bother touching it. He chose instead to earn his money back through the stock market than by attempting to retrieve it through feculence.

  Anton's family believed he paid his bills by picking up odd tech jobs off Linked-In and coding for small start-ups. The only legitimate position he'd held was in 2018, writing a cute, little algorithm for an Indian YouTube account that showcased music videos that wished to increase its subscriber count. They found immense success directly after and continue to grow.

Anton spent his time as a highly-respected conspiracy theorist blogger on the dark web. On one occasion, he'd been approached by the FBI offering well-paid employment, but he rejected their offer. His issue was that they wanted to cage an otherwise free bird. They were going to force him to sit in an office for forty hours a week under observation and follow their rules. He envisioned the government holding him captive between four sterile walls, wearing stiff, strangling clothes with too many buttons pinching his wrists and neck and corduroy pants. Give me death before you give me corduroy was his motto in life. With his sensory integration, touching that material felt like an electrical shock. No, thank you. Worst of all, they had regulations. He would have to follow their unspoken code of conduct like an alien robot. He'd be forced to walk to the water cooler for a sip of water while he smiled at strangers. The very idea triggered his nervous tics. They would consider his supervision a matter of national security if they divulged their undercover operations to him. Amusingly, he already knew all of their secrets, and he didn't care about a single one of them. What did concern him? Major injustice, the welfare of the planet, his new chihuahua, and, come the holidays, family. He always hoped to find his family safe in their farmhouse in Texas, sitting around a beautiful conifer just waiting for him to make an appearance, relieved to find that he had stayed out of harm's way and out of prison. Well, mostly. There was that one situation in 2017. However, it was never pursued. As soon as the warrant was issued for his arrest, it vanished, lost in cyberspace. Imagine that!

Putting his Jeep into gear, he pulled away from the curb and glanced in his rear-view mirror with a smug look, nodding at himself after seeing no one on his trail. After picking up speed, he noticed that his passenger tire sounded like it had a bit of a limp. He drove cautiously another block or two, making a few turns to find a discreet location, and pulled over. He rolled his eyes when he saw that his tire had quickly lost air. Ugh! Real-world problems, he lamented. He opened the driver's door to pop the latch to release his trunk when suddenly, the lights went out. There was a bag over his head, arms flailing, and he was thrown off-balance by his attackers. The second before losing consciousness, he realized that he had finally been bested. Bastards! Was his fleeting thought as his body went limp, defeated, and two gentlemen of formidable stature quickly hoisted his wiry frame into an unmarked SUV.

CHAPTER SEVEN

BONNIE BARONESS

THE MARQUEZ FAMILY had arrived in Galveston to embark on a Caribbean cruise. They were boarding the ship and looking forward to a day of swimming and playing in the water park before the boat left the port. The youngest of the three girls, Paulina, was most excited as this was her first see faring excursion. As Thalia's eyes ran over what appeared to be thousands of cabin windows, Wendy eyed the giant lettering on the ship's stern, Bonnie Baroness, she mouthed.

"What's a Baroness?" she asked her parents.

"Robert, what's a baroness?" Priscilla asked of her husband, slapping him on the back, having the knowledge yet unsure how to explain it exactly.

"And who's Bonnie," asked Paulina.

"Ow!" he said, holding his shoulder in mock pain, shifting away from his attacker, beer bottles clanking in his bag, amused smirk lurking. "A baroness is like a queen but not quite. She was like a lord's wife back when they had kings and queens and everything. Actually, she was a baron's wife who was a big landowner in charge of the serfs in the region." he explained to their middle daughter. "Bonnie just means pretty," he said to the youngest. Priscilla rolled her eyes at his simple yet accurate explanation loving him but hating him for gaining superiority when it came to the worship in their children's eyes. Mostly, she loved him.

The first day at sea was a glorious gluttonous event. There was no shortage of food or entertainment; the ocean and its inhabitants were incredible. If you were near the edge, you could see fish and other entities swimming below. Lounging poolside, Priscilla recorded the girls playing from her phone. Wendy laid out a towel, lazily eying the teenage boy across the pool. She was doing a poor job of pretending to be watching videos on her phone through the darkened lens of her sunglasses. The two younger girls were wrestling over a giant, yellow flamingo float in the pool. The winner of the match, Thalia, mounted it proudly and put her fists in the air, proclaiming her victory. Paulina dove underwater crouched at the bottom of the pool, and performed an epic power plunge in which she emerged between her sister's legs knocking her backward and under the water. Thalia's scream of surprise was muffled by the water flooding her mouth as the usurped toppled backward. Having stolen the mount of the flamingo she'd named Geoffrey the Pink, Paulina paddled her legs clockwise, turning her newly acquired vehicle 180 degrees so she was face-to-face with the loser. Thalia stood in the shallow end, hair plastered over her face, rubbing the back of her head where she's knocked it. Without warning, she dropped below the top of the water and then popped up long enough to spit out a fountain of water right into Paulina's face!

"Sicko! Paulina shrieked and began

paddling after her. Laughing, Thalia somersaulted backward and underneath the water, where she swam to the deep end and sat cross-legged on the pool floor, appearing to meditate only by releasing bubbles every 30 seconds or so. Bored after realizing she'd lost despite her victory, Paulina paddled off to the shallow end, pulling her Hello Kitty shades down over her eyes and waving farewell to all the kids without the luxury of a raft. Priscilla slapped Robert making him spill his brand new Corona.

"Are you watching this?" she asked her husband.

"Watching what?" he asked, completely perplexed, flicking the puddle of beer out of his crotch.

"Aye, aye, aye." She chided.

"What?" he asked in deeper confusion. She waved her arm in surrender.

"Never mind," she grumbled. He put both palms up, bemused, and took another swig enjoying the breeze. She laughed. After lunch, Wendy wandered off and was visiting quietly with Nic-from-Cancun on the ship's bow.

"Yeah, I totally saw you by the pool and thought you were hot." said the gray-eyed Nicolas with his right hand playing nervously in his nut-brown waves.

"What? You saw me? No way!" she responded in feigned surprise.

"Yeah. I was gonna talk to you, but I think your mom was there, and you were on your phone but you're hot. Are you 18?" he asked pointedly.

"What are they doing?" Wendy said, looking over his shoulder. She put her hand over her face. Across the deck, the pretty girl observed little sisters reenacting the scene from Titanic where Rose's heart decides to go on and on. Immediately losing interest in the boy, she jogged off. "You guys are idiots!" she yelled at them, laughing, abandoning the boring conversation without a goodbye.

"Hey, but what's your name? I'm Nic! I'm from Cancun!" he called after her.

"Paulina! Get down from there!" Priscilla scolded, noticing all three of her girls way too close to the edge. Unsticking herself from her plastic seat, she rose to retrieve her children when, from her vantage point, their performance went from humorous to dangerous.

"Look, Mama!" the youngest pointed at some animals breaking the surf.

"Dolphins!" announced Thalia delightedly.

"Mija, those aren't dolphins. That's a pod of whales," their mother corrected just as her husband walked up, putting hands on his wife's shoulders, taking in the salty sea air and the incredible view.

"What's wrong with them?" he wondered aloud. "Is that normal for them to jump out of the water like that?"

"Yes, Tonto! Haven't you ever seen videos of them doing that? I sent you that video on Facebook. You didn't even watch it, did you?" she accused.

"Which video? You send me lots of videos." he said in defense. She raised a hand to smack him playfully, but he blocked the strike and beat her to the punchline with a kiss on the forehead.

Suddenly, they were knocked off balance as hair-raising sounds emanated from the water.

"What was that?" asked a mom with a toddler on her hip approaching the railing.

"We couldn't really see," explained Robert craning to scan the water. The whales were nowhere to be seen. "Maybe that was some kind of echolocation thing?" he speculated aloud, trying to calm his nervous family.

"I'm going to TikTok this," said Paulina pulling out her iPhone. Suddenly the ship quaked, and the phone tumbled overboard. After a loud splash, the video feed went black.

CHAPTER EIGHT

STRAWBERRY PRESERVE

EVELYN DABBED RAW honey over toast and sipped the full-bodied coffee she'd brewed from freshly ground beans from the Blackbird Café off of Orange Avenue, transfixed by the hypnotic surf pounding the beach from atop the weathered deck. This was the Redwood balcony that the she and her husband had constructed with their own two hands. She teared up but smiled at the memory of them knocking over the gallon of wood stain gallon as they made love under the stars after witnessing a spectacular sunset. Scraped, exhausted, sun-kissed, and in love, they laughed as he rolled them strategically, carefully guiding her golden flesh clear of the spill without uncoupling.

However, this morning sitting alone, the breeze blowing the edges of her hair, tickled her back from bittersweet recollection. Slouchy sweater sagging off her slender shoulder, her polished toes outstretched to rest on the mismatched footstool, she stared into the melodious sea contemplatively.

She'd had a restless night. The excitement of the event in the lab had been troubled by indecision. Despite the night's passage, she had remained awestruck and ill at ease about what to do next. She was sure of one thing; She needed to confer with a colleague. Whom she couldn't decide. She had never developed a deep rapport with her peers at work because she'd always worked alongside Adem. For the most part, the couple kept to themselves. Other than her marriage, Evelyn focused on her research and her students rather than forming interpersonal relationships. She was perfectly friendly to those surrounding them; however, she was indifferent to outsiders of the unassailable domain shared between her and her mate. For so long, she'd been partnered with her spouse, fellow researcher, and best friend. The two spent their days and nights together, reveling in discovery and fulfilling their dreams. Their work hours were filled with wide-eyed teaching pupils, in-depth inquiry in the lab, and their nights and weekends with passionate leisure. At least, they were until the incident last year. That was a day not soon forgotten.

Her fingers brushed the remnant of scars on her hands from the burns and the fading pink jagged blight that was a reminder on her forehead. She was glad she was unconscious when it was stitched back together. The scar had grown silvery and mostly smooth now.

Her eyes fell downcast knowing there was only one researcher she favored for this sensitive job. Still, she also knew that entrusting him would breach their unspoken agreement of solidarity against one another. She hated to appear needy, especially after how vulnerable she'd proved to be in their marriage, but this was bigger than them; this was science. She uncurled from her settee and walked indoors to retrieve her phone. She glanced at the analog clock which kept vigil in the dining room.

It's 7:30 on Saturday morning. Can't you just wait until tomorrow when he comes by to drop off Kanik? she thought to herself. *Swallow your pride, you damned fool. We have the whole weekend ahead of us. Why waste it? Time may be of the essence here!* She battled her wit and her sense of pride in this futile battle.

She shook her head at her obstinate thinking and searched her phone for the contact "Beast." She hadn't had the heart to change it after he substituted his name in her phone listing Beauty for her name in his phone as a private joke years ago. Not often overtly romantic, he sometimes did small things that tenderly nurtured her innermost thoughts and desires. Of all people, it was he who knew her best. That was one thing she loved. That was one of the million things he did that made her sure he was her better half. She typed "Beast" and scrolled to the log of their correspondence. Since the split, it had been nothing but cordial meeting times to exchange the dog. No tenderness. No concessions. With that realization, she put the phone down, feeling defeated. Resembling a young girl instead of a grown woman, she folded up at the dining room table, tucked her hair behind her ear, and gnawed her bottom lip. Lost deep in thought, she called upon her richly scientific brain.

Who's the best candidate for a research partner in this case? Consider the following factors: experience, education, work ethic, intelligence, and trustworthiness. Indignant but acquiescent, she had her answer. With newfound insight, she picked up her phone, moved to dial, and then recanted. Instead, she composed the following text message:

"I must see you today. Come here for brunch at 10:00 am. regarding a scientific matter of great urgency." As she always did, she proofread her message and hit send, after which she sat astonished by her sudden exhilaration.

He is coming here. Today. For a social visit. Well, not actually, but she supposed it kind of was since it was for more than a dog exchange. Excitedly, she picked up her phone checking. No response yet. Well, it had only been one second. My gosh! She needed a shower, she realized, and maybe a haircut! *No! Don't start all that again.* She chided herself. *Just be cool. Don't go overboard,* she told herself, squealing as she ran up the stairs to take bathe.

Knowing that she had time, she took a

long, hot shower, untangling stiff muscles, and dressed carefully in an attempt to relax. Overcome with elation, she tousled her hair and pinned it up carelessly. She ran to the market for fresh fruit, bread, and maybe some deli meats. When she arrived at the store, she'd realized he had yet to confirm their appointment. Sitting in her car, her intestines tightened as she pulled her phone out of her bag.

Yes. He has responded. she noted. *Of course, he had. It had been over an hour now.* She opened the message. It read:

"Can't. I have a date." Heat rose to her face and her eyes flooded.

"Then you can just rot in hell, you j-a-c-" she was in the progress of typing when she got another message. She paused and clicked it open.

"JK. See you in 30", it read.

"Jackass!" She finished aloud and then deleted the whole message. Oh my gosh. I have no words for that man. Stay focused now! Still rattled, she settled herself and got out of her car to continue her errand. She rushed through the store, picking up everything on her list except grape jelly. Instead, she grabbed some strawberry and swiftly checked out, knowing that her Adem only ate a grape. She drove home hastily, and her breath caught in her chest when she pulled up to see him lounging on the deck; Kanik wagging with enthusiasm, waiting for his master to throw a stick off the balcony.

Adem faked two hearty throws trying to test the dog's wits and laughed raucously when the dog flinched, looked but didn't budge. She heard him praise the dog for his intelligence and then stood up and hurled that heavy stick an extraordinary length, the muscles in his upper body rippling noticeably under his t-shirt. She noticed she was holding her breath, but it was knocked out of her lungs when Kanik yipping manically clambered passed her down the stairs nearly knocking her down. His quest was to search for his new favorite toy. Struggled now between her purse, keys and the grocery bags she ascended the stairs, trying to quiet her pounding heart at the sight of her husband behaving so amiably. It made her flush with fervor even though it was only toward the dog and not her. Adem came down the steps, two at a time, and, although he didn't greet her verbally, lifted the heavy canvas bags off her shoulders and walked ahead of her unlocking the door and holding it open for her, which was classic Adem. Ignore typical convention but act like a real gentleman where it counts. She noted, hiding a smirk riddled with irritation and joyful familiarity.

She enjoyed how he took care of her when it mattered. She appreciated that he was there to take the weight off her shoulders. That was what he did for her, in so many ways. Although he sometimes made her howling mad, he always looked out for her when it mattered. He challenged her, too, not just in some inanimate Ken doll. He was a real man with his own thoughts, beliefs, and opinions. It was more only natural that they didn't always agree. All of those thoughts raced through her mind in the five seconds it took her to climb the last few steps and duck underneath his bulging forearm and into the kitchen.

"So... Hello! ... Good morning?" she flustered awkwardly.

"Hi. Yeah. So, what's up?" he quipped.

"Oh! So, no breakfast. Just straight to business?" she bristled, feeling foolish that she unwittingly expected this meeting would be more somehow.

"Well, I'll eat. You should eat. So, yes, let's have breakfast, but your message was... out of the blue and offered no explanation. Are you okay?" he asked. "What happened?" he asked pointedly. Adem stopped unbagging the groceries and turned to look her square in the face.

"Well, yes." she blushed, realizing it might have been her who was possibly being slightly irrational. "It's big!" she began, motioning with her hands, then putting her hands on her hips defiantly, trying to regain control of the situation, choosing to keep her secret veiled at least for a few minutes. "I'm starving, for the record." He gazed at her with interest, his eyes wide. Noticing that she was enjoying this attention and bit of power play, he watched her, curious. "I'll need time to tell the whole account from beginning to end, and I want breakfast, so I said we should meet for brunch. So, let's eat." she drew out, lacking her typical eloquence, still giving him no indication of the purpose of their meeting. He shrugged, never one to turn down a meal, and went back to unpacking groceries.

"Your hand!" he brushed her arm, taking note of the fresh bandage.

"I'm fine. That's all part of it," she said. "Believe me. This was too big just for me," she admitted, half-smiling in glee at the enormity of her announcement but more by the touch of his hand and his evident expression of concern.

"All right." he relented. Having pulled out freshly baked loaves of rye and sourdough bread from the sack, his and her favorites from the corner grocery store, his stomach cramped in anticipation. He'd not been focused on eating well in the last few months. Adem opened the fridge in search of garnish. He had already spotted her local honey on the counter.

"Grape?" he asked, rummaging through the spotless, nearly empty refrigerator at a loss.

"No. I'm out. I have strawberry." she

offered, pulling the fresh jar from the bag. He turned around knowing she did not partake in jellies, jams, or preserves, even if her life depended on it. She did not need strawberry as no one in this house ate strawberry, especially him.

"Is this for your new boyfriend?" he asked, squaring his shoulders in mock anger.

"No. It's for you to throw at your pretty, little date," she admitted in resignation, knowing she'd been blatantly caught in a passive-aggressive act. It had seemed so much more passive than aggressive while in the store, but, in hindsight, the purchase was a petty act of vengeance.

"My *date* was Dr. Smith with Kanik. He has another ear infection. I was supposed to see him at 9:30, but they squeezed us in earlier when I told them you needed tending."

Peeved, "Another ear infection!" she exclaimed, trying to divert the attention away from her foolishness, flooding with relief.

"Yes. He needs a round of antibiotic drops just like before. It's no big deal." He responded calmly and coolly, which was typical of him. She walked over to the big bay window and smiled, watching Kanik jumping and barking at a tree, challenging a giant squirrel in no danger of being caught by him ever. That wily squirrel was fearless and seemed to enjoy the game, teasing the massive dog daily, chittering at him with one fuzzy paw, hurling her worst insults. Evelyn beamed at this turn of events, hugging herself, knowing that this scenario could be happening again every morning if things just worked out.

"So, I guess I'll have cereal and fruit. You?" he inquired.

"Coffee," she replied. He turned away from the pantry, aborting his search for grape jelly, and stared at her recalling her big proclamation about her massive appetite but then laughed. "And fruit!" she amended. "I've been dying for a grapefruit!" she clarified. He rolled his eyes and sat down with his cereal, waiting quietly for her to spill the beans after a meager attempt at small talk that began with her mocking his recent professional endeavors.

"So, any new developments in the Jesus Christ Division?" He raised one eyebrow appearing anything but charmed. He sat, chewing in silence, choosing not to engage in her banter. When her poor-humored diversion was met with a total lack of applause, she stopped deviating and explained the events of the previous day moment by moment. He nodded now and then, encouraging her when she began the discussion earnestly and meeting her gaze when she slowed down to check in and make sure he was still listening. Finally, after each event had correctly been recounted and he'd taken a moment to digest the information, he spoke.

"Why the right cheek? And why only tattoo one side?"

"Really? That's what you are choosing to comment on?" she stood and approached his side of the table. She charged him, eyes flashing in hot anger mixed with charming amusement, reminded of how funny he could be, hands outstretched as if to strangle him. His large hands encircled her wrists, and he pulled her face close to his. Now chest to chest with her hands pinned, totally defenseless, they stood motionless, breathing hard. Although he was taller than her by eight inches, her lips were irresistibly close. He kissed her. Just a quick peck and then sat back down and resumed eating, pausing to submerge his grape nuts in the pool of milk and then, in sincerity, asked,

"How could you sit on this all night, Evie? I was on campus. You could have picked up your office phone and dialed my extension. I could have been there in fifteen minutes!" he responded reasonably, then pulled out the chair next to him and patted it, inviting her to sit at his side. With flushed cheeks, she sat feeling warm and genuinely acknowledged. They finished their food, picking at it here and there while unraveling the scientific implications for hours: debating, reflecting, bouncing ideas and potential consequences off of each other, designing theories, and deflating them as the hours slid by.

They soon discovered that it was late into the night and that they were famished. Surprised by how heavily immersed they had become, Kanik wagged in thanks as she poured his kibble. Seeing how happy the dog was, Adem dialed their favorite place for Sushi and ordered both of their favorite dishes to be delivered so they could continue refueled and unabated.

They took turns speaking and listening, drawing sketches, and pulling books, old and new, from their library for reference. At one point in the night, she balanced, perched on top of the mantle with her hands splayed and hair flying wildly, reenacting the part of when the ravenous jellyfish devoured her blood, and he sat with a finger over his mouth, trying not to spit out his popcorn. Raising a hand to speak, in interruption of her epiphany as if he had reached a level of higher consciousness,

"So, this species is currently known as *Turritopsis dohrnii*?" he asked in confirmation.

"Yes, but I mean, that was based on the idea of them being a unique jellyfish, an eternal bottom feeder. Not some shape shifting carnivore."

"Exactly. So, the species needs a new name."

"Well, I would think so. Maybe, *Humboldtei*? Usually, a species is renamed when such a profound discovery is made. I think this justifies a whole new genus. Maybe the Genus should be *Evelenei*." she agreed, thinking aloud. Standing abruptly, one finger in the air. Kanik slid from his lap, landing with a soft thud.

"I've got it!" he proclaimed.

"What?" she hopped. "What shall we call them?"

"It will ring simple but true. *Turds*!"

"What? No!" she jumped up laughing and climbed him like a tree to kiss his lips, his whole body shaking with laughter. She then pulled out her Genus *Turritopsis* book and began to list the other species: *Turritopsis* is a genus of hydrozoans in the family *Oceaniidae: chevalense, inquirenda, fascicularis, lata Lendenfeld*," she looked up to discover that she was, in fact, reading to the dog. "Hey, where'd you go?" she called.

"Peeing. I can still hear you though. Go on!" he shouted from the bathroom.

"Well, there's *minor* and *nutricula*, *pacifica*, *pleurostoma*, *polycirrha*, and *finally rubra*. Are you sure you can hear me?" she yelled louder than before.

"Yes," he said quietly, walking back into the room. "But you didn't mention the turds." To prove that he had, in fact, heard the entire list. "And you know what's funny. At the end of their lifespan, they turn into a polyp. Do you see a theme here?" He asked her with a ridiculous grin, surreptitiously joyful at seeing his old wife again, the passionate woman he'd fallen for long ago. She grabbed his biceps and tried shaking him in exasperation. He didn't budge.

"Not turds and now we know they do not even turn into polyps."

"I mean, they sound like little assholes to me," he continued, not relenting. He held up her injury, reminding her of what she'd witnessed of the little creature just one day prior. "Imagine if you have put your finger in the water." She leaped up in excitement, pretending to beat his chest with tiny fists in exasperation but laughed playfully. Truly unique was this woman he was married to, he silently mused. After this ruckus of the turd debacle finally wound down, the more intense dance of the intellects deepened as they discussed the implications of her discovery for hours until he fell asleep next to her on the couch.

Adem awoke a few hours later with a kink in his neck and rose wearily to don his shoes to head to the apartment but paused. A tiny smile touched his mouth when he saw she'd reached for him in her sleep once his warmth left the couch. His dimples flashed in surrender, and instead of putting on his kicks, he scooped her up and carried her upstairs to bed. He pulled off her shoes and joggers and gently unfastened her earrings. Just as he knew she did when she was tired, he carefully laid her clothes over the armchair and set her mother of pearl earrings into her jewelry box just where they belonged. He shrugged out of his clothing, casting it down to the floor, slipping underneath the flaxen bedding next to her. She mewled and rolled his direction, searching hands outstretched, and he wondered if she'd done this every night since he'd gone away. Knowing their separation was behind them, he curled his arms around her and pulled her into his chest. Drooling ever so slightly, she nestled into him, purring.

The next morning, she woke with a start in Adem's arms, where she'd only dreamt of being for months. Puzzled for a split second, the memories of all that transpired came crashing back to her. She quietly covered her hand with her mouth, grinning feverishly. Needing a moment to take in the scene, she laid back again. The whole world seemed brighter and more beautiful. Her movement has roused him slightly. He rolled over with his back to her. She ever so gently reached her small delicate hands over his trapezius, scapula, and shoulder blades, ever fascinated with the tone and brawn of his body. She took her hand back and took a few deep breaths soaking up the view. She grinned, mulling over this new development in her life: her marriage back on track, a new scientific discovery, and ... strawberry jelly that needed to be donated to whoever was willing to eat it in the lounge at work. Squeezing her eyes shut, she sat up, trying to process the turn of events. After some simple stretches out on the balcony, she quietly grabbed her yoga mat and patted back into the bedroom.

Evelyn was delighted to see him still in their bed, shirtless. She scooted back into the bed and took a moment to watch him breathing peacefully, his robust chest rising and falling. He kicked the blankets off while sleeping deeply. She admired the red ink on his muscular shoulder written there years ago in her honor. She was tempted to trace it with her finger but chose to leave him alone to not further risk waking him.

"Totus tuus," it read. *Totally yours* in Latin to represent their eternal love for one another founded in the most academic languages, a dead language, which would live forever through their intertwined lives and studies. It matched the inscription on her ribcage, her proclamation of forever to him. "My beautiful beast," she murmured. She rose, feeling rejuvenated and relaxed, despite getting so few hours of shuteye. She grinned at Kanik, snoring loudly as he hung off his too-small cot at the foot of their four-poster bed. She knew this was the start of a wild journey, but she would be safe no matter what because she had the good doctor by her side, and, once again, he had her.

CHAPTER NINE

GUAM

AFTER A 20-HOUR, direct flight, Alex landed at Guam International Airport looking as freshly pressed and presentable as he did the previous morning despite his sleep deprivation and the stifling humidity. It had gone from Saturday before dawn to dusk on Sunday, thanks to a long day of travel plus a fourteen-hour time change. His first destination was Guam Regional Medical City in Dededo, where the singular survivor of the incident was being treated. Although in a coma, he needed to lay eyes on this man and reassess the situation.

When he emerged from the baggage bay

and exited GIA, he was surprised to see a small row of yellow taxis available on the street, which looked commercial enough as Guam is a tourist destination, he reminded himself. You never know what to expect when you travel abroad. One of the cars pulled out into the lane and waved him over. The driver threw the gearshift in park mid-lane and jumped out to open the door for his passenger. Alex greeted the driver.

"Hospital, please." handing the driver a printout of the written address and was puzzled when he responded with,

"Yes, Sir, Mr. Joe, Sir." Alex' brow furrowed for just a moment but then said thank you. As the car sped off, he was surprised to see the city looking deserted. Well, abandoned but asleep with all the restaurants and shops appearing closed. The driver noticed his observation and offered an explanation,

"Church day! Rest Day!" he grinned. It was Sunday night. After which, he noticed an obscene amount of ornate little churches along the way. He saw a few people lazily mulling around a grassy area in the falling light of day but other than that, the city appeared bedded down. The trip was speedy and relatively uneventful. Alex dozed for a few minutes, his head bobbing for the second half of the drive, but he came to attention without aid as he felt the car come to a jarring halt in front of GRMC and was pleased to see an impressive, five-story hospital that looked to be a new build, no more than five years old.

"Thank you, Driver," he said, nodding

and handing up his fare plus a twenty-dollar tip which the driver took with hesitation.

He disembarked and realized that it might have been prudent to check into his room because now he had to carry his luggage into the hospital. Still, haste seemed more important than appearances, especially since the man was reported to be in a coma. He could probably crawl into the bed and nap on top of the guy for all he would care. He didn't think that Tracy was the guy's name, would mind if he carried a few bags.

He entered the hospital and looked for any staff on duty. Although it appeared relatively luxurious, no one seemed to be attending the front counter. His mind rewound about 15 seconds to the group of staff he observed smoking and socializing by the dumpster in scrubs and assumed that one of those lovely ladies may be the front desk clerk on a shift break. Live tropical plants were adorning the walls and countertops, and one cross-looking maintenance worker watering them looked up but offered no assistance. A flatscreen on the counter showcased a news anchor talking to a young man in a sports uniform, seeming to interview him with statistics scrolling across the bottom of the screen. A loud waterfall splashed in the foyer, and Alex looked around again. The maintenance worker continued to scowl directly at him.

"Now, to you, Stephanie." The silver-haired gentleman on the screen said to the young, fresh-faced anchor. "Thank you, Jeff." She said, looking pleasant but appropriately alarmed by the telling of the upcoming event. Taking another look around, Alex did see that the signs were all in English. He spied one that read, "Intensive Care Unit" and figured that that hall seemed as good as any. As he crouched to retrieve his belongings, a small voice resonated from the front doors. A woman of tiny stature, not exceeding four foot nine, with a very full figure. She toddled by him and behind the counter, nearly disappearing. She smoothed her hair, tucking a few unruly strands back into a massive bun taking up her post behind the counter, never breaking eye contact with him. She tucked a small cigarette purse under the counter and into a drawer.

"Welcome to Guam Regional Medical City, Dededo, where we offer world-class medical care to the residents of Guam and the CNMI, Palau, the FSM, and the Marshall Islands, including all of Micronesia. Our Specialty Clinics include Cardiology, Oncology/Hematology, Hyperbaric Wound Care, Neurology, Orthopedics, Pulmonology, Infectious Disease Control, and other departments like Radiology, Patient Education, Physical Medicine & Rehabilitation and Emergency." She took a long breath and added a disarming smile. "How may I help you?". He smiled in return, suddenly refreshed by her energy. He'd found her performance entertaining and her strong command of the language reassuring. Furthermore, he felt that she would be more than adequate to guide him in the direction he needed.

"Yes. I hope you can. I am seeking an American patient named Tracy John. Can you tell me where I might find him? He was admitted yesterday after a terrible accident at sea and sadly is in deplorable condition." he elaborated with almost all of the information at his disposal.

"Tracy John? Can you tell me his date of birth, Sir?" she inquired as her very long fingernails made a pleasant little clicking sound on the surface of a flatscreen monitor at the reception station.

"I can. Give me a moment," he responded as he walked away from his luggage and approached the counter with his briefcase, encapsulating his reports.

"No need, Sir. I have found him. He is in the Intensive Care Unit in bed 16." she clicked pleasantly out of the program, looking up at him from under long, dark lashes. "That's a private room," she added, dazzling him with another warm smile.

"Do you need to see my ID?" he offered, in no hurry to pick up his heavy bags and walk down a long corridor to stare at some vegetable at the behest of his employer.

"No, Sir. The hospital campus is open to the public as we treat many outpatients and their families, but you will be asked to show identification on the floor before you are granted access to the patient's room. The hall you need is… right that way." she responded as she walked out from behind the counter and pointed down the hall he initially intended to go down. He nodded in appreciation, now feeling waited on adequately, and commenced.

After proving his identity and his intended business concerning the patient at the nurse's station, he was granted access to room 16. He was surprised to see an attendant dropping off dinner to an upright patient who appeared quite lively and spoke Tagalog to the worker. Alex stepped back and double-checked the room number and confirmed the number. Slightly puzzled, he entered.

"I'm Alexander Becker, Quality control, Safety, and Environmental Manager of Dominion Petroleum Corporation, looking for Tracy John?" he began.

"I am him," he said in English adorned in a heavy accent.

"I'm happy to see you looking so well." he held out a hand and shook hands with the tentative young man, approaching one of the chairs at the bedside. Tracy weakly returned the shake and nodded toward the chair, granting permission for him to sit.

"I am alive. No one else is," he responded. "So, I guess I am more than well."

"Yes. It was reported to the corporate that you were... incapacitated."

"I am not." He testified.

"Yes." Alex agreed apologetically, deliberately not using phrases containing the word sorry because that could be misconstrued as an admission of guilt or negligence. "Can you tell me what your position was on the rig?" he queried, poised over a legal pad with a ballpoint pen in hand. Tracy looked over the bed rail at this man, conveying a severe lack of faith in his superior.

"Don't you know this? I was the lead

geologist assigned to semi-submersible platform K. The reports I had studied indicated that this site was safe for drilling. The reports were wrong, the trench was not safe!" he illuminated, indignation rising in his voice. "I had recruited my little brother to come and work on that barge. He had only joined me two weeks ago. I was so busy prepping for the first drill that I had only seen him once."

"I understand that you feel loss, Mr. John. May I get the name of your brother and his position?" The air hung heavily between them. Alex waited and hoped that his meeting would not be fruitless; he didn't have any words that felt appropriate to say to this young man who had fought so hard on behalf of the Dominion cause, and what it cost the man was truly immeasurable. He felt an intense desire to be less professional and be present on behalf of mankind, not the firm; however, duty called, and he remained silent.

Tracy lifted the dome covering his entrée and shook his head when he saw the food choice.

"Kelaguen uhang," he said in frustration. When this didn't seem to register with the businessman man, the younger man explained, "This is a dish of shrimp and prawns."

"Not your favorite?" Alex guessed.

"I'm deathly allergenic to shellfish. I'm the only survivor of the explosion, and the hospital staff just almost murdered me in my nurse bed! What kind of hospital is this place?" he sat forward, grimacing, trying to look out into the hall to discover what was going on outside of his area.

"Explosion?" Alex asked with interest and then changed his tone. "Can I get you something else to eat? They have a cafeteria. What would you like?" he offered good-naturedly as if maybe a crusty cafeteria meal that was not fatal to this lone survivor might cure all his ails. Just then, the phone in the room rang. His hands balled up into fists as he looked over his shoulder, realizing that his IV cord was tethering him too closely to his sickbed to allow him to answer the phone.

"Allow me." Alex offered to pick up the large, canary yellow receiver. "Hello. Room of Tracy John. May I help you?"

"Kapatid? Buhay ka pa? Big brother, umiiyak si mom!" said a frantic girl on the other end of the line.

"Uh… It's for you." Becker said. He said,

covering the receiver, "What would you like for dinner? I'll go while you talk." he suggested politely.

"Adobo." Answered Tracy dismissively. "Please, give me the phone," he said with one wave dismissing the strange man while he began his conversation with a welcome familiar voice.

"Masama ang pakiramdam ko, Angel. Ang sakit ng ulo ko." Pulling the phone away from his ear, he said, "My brother's name was Jasir." and then resumed his conversation with his sister. Alex frowned in receipt of that information, noting that the young man was likely giving the news of Jasir's death to a family member. He knew that Dominion did not have an accurate roster of the fatalities. Alex was surprised to find upon his phone call that Jasir was not anywhere on that roster and that they were only updated to the cloud monthly. There were possibly up to 200 bodies lost at sea that they had no account of. While he searched the cafeteria, he called the home office.

"I was told this guy was an American laborer," Alex argued with the woman in records.

"He's from Manila, but he has an American Visa."

"And he's a scientist, not a laborer."

"Everyone who works on the marine barge is listed as a laborer except the foremen. They are coded by pay grade. Everyone on the platform was on a pay scale 'G,' except for the foreman and service workers," she explained unapologetically. With no further information than before, he concluded his call and tried to order some adobe for Tracy. None could be found, so he settled for a turkey sandwich, a fruit bowl, and a strawberry frappe. Who doesn't love strawberry? He went back to the ICU with his spoils, hoping the snacks would lighten the mood. Tracy was off of the phone and ready to talk. Alex noticed the man's swollen red eyes and the tissues on the bed and felt genuine sorrow.

"There are things you need to know," Tracy said as he reached for the food.

"They didn't have any adobe." Alex explained with a slight frown as he handed Tracy and the food, "and the kitchen was closed down, but they did have some prepackaged stuff, and a barista was on duty. No shellfish!" He promised hands raised palm up as if in a stickup. Tracy shook his head in mild disgust at this man's lack of cultural awareness and stated the following.

"Get out your notepad." he opened the dry sandwich wrapper and sipped noisily on the frappe. "On 'D' Day, the day of the explosion, I was out on a dingy about half a mile from the drilling site pulling some samples. For the last three months, the marine team has assembled the drill below with the new machinery. Do you know anything about the Mariana Trench?" He asked. Alex opened his mouth to reply but didn't have anything groundbreaking to reveal, so he chose not to speak. The scientist continued. "This place has been less explored than the moon. It's an amazing mystery, geologically speaking and otherwise. It's like a scar in the Earth's crust that is deeper than Mount Everest is tall. Since it's become a Marine National Monument, I don't even see how you were able to get permission to drill for crude oil there." he digressed in disgust. Alex held up a hand to interject.

"I do know that. See, not the whole trench is protected, and we agreed to finance some environmental research, which might have been why you were there," Alex supplied. Tracy cut him off.

"I was watching the team because when the drill started, the whole surface of the water began to vibrate. I watched the seven men directly above the site on a boat with monitors gauging the depth of the drills. Most of everyone else was out on the platform watching. This day was one we had all worked toward for the last eighteen months together. We had just completed the connection of the main umbilicus the week before. You know every face on the rig when you work and live with the same 500 people for over a year. It should've taken about five hours to breach the crust, but after about one minute of boring, the explosion occurred. That was the apparent moment of impact, of what, I don't know. I was knocked unconscious and nearly drowned by a huge explosion. Luckily, I had a life jacket and was tethered to my boat. When I awoke afloat near my vessel, I observed the men in the boat were in the air on top of a huge geyser. Parts of their bodies and boat were just up there for a while. Everyone on the barge was watching and yelling. A second boom sounded and created a massive tidal wave.

This caused the barge to tip and bob on the water, and then I started hearing explosions from up there, and I watched in disbelief when it began to catch fire."

'Two blasts, fire on the platform,' Alex scrawled.

"I watched in horror as men and women jumped to their deaths. I heard their screams as some burned to death and watched some of them being splattered out over the water as a series of explosions blew up one after another. I sat, horrified, knowing that they were all lost, including Jasir. I also knew that I was not likely to ever be found. Then, last night I was found unconscious several miles from the scene. Someone picked up in a…" he struggled for the word, "jet, and brought to the doctors here. I don't know how that happened, but

I've been thinking about what went wrong since then."

So, I figured that the drills must have punctured a cavern that we didn't know about, which created a vacuum, which may have caused the geyser. I believe that the blast created a wave that caused the gas lines to rupture. Next, the compression tanks on the rig burst. When those ignited, it caused a chain reaction. Because of my location, I was blown clear of the central region of destruction and floated relatively unharmed until I was discovered." He stopped talking for a moment and wiped his eyes. His voice began to break at this point. "I had hesitated to take this position because I'm not specifically a marine geologist, but the money was good. I planned to marry my fiancé this fall, and this money would have gone a long way toward our honeymoon. My working theory is that this pocket was created by magma at least three million years ago that had cooled too quickly and formed this pocket. Due to the intense pressure of the cavern, it was believed that retrieving it would take less energy, but the immense release of the pressure was not predicted to be so violent. Our calculations were partially based on estimated factors. That was all a working theory as no one had harvested oil from so deep in the ocean before. There was no way to know what would happen for sure." He looked up at Alex and noticed him checking his phone to make sure his phone was still recording.

"Invaluable information." he proffered, holding up the phone.

"While I was watching that water tunnel, I noted…. some gelatinous forms emerging. They flowed with the water and then spread out across the water like a plasma. They didn't have a shape. At first, I thought they were the liquefied remains of some undiscovered animal, maybe a species of Ulmaridae, but I saw the membranes forming groups. They didn't have any distinct body parts but appeared to be drawn to each other almost magnetically. Before the second blast, I observed a few different masses forming. This was like nothing I've ever seen before; we may have transported a new species from the depths up to the surface. I don't see how it could survive up top if it's biologically designed for life on the ocean floor, but if you mess with nature, you can be surprised by the results. Who knows, maybe it's a top predator of amoeba and other micro-life in the depths of the trench. We should try to document their progress... or their demise." he remarked, straw gurgling as he fished the last few chunks of ice from his frappe.

"Well, that was a lot of information!" Alex exclaimed with raised eyebrows. "First and foremost, I am glad that you do appear, alive. Secondly, how much of this account would you feel was indisputable fact? Would you say there were two separate blasts?" Alex pressed. Tracy shrugged in disbelief.

"You know, I'm exhausted. I don't really want to talk anymore today," he said, laying back in his bed. He raised his head as Nurse Jones entered the room.

"Sir, I'm so sorry but our visiting hours

are over now. You may come tomorrow." The blond nurse instructed. She stood there stiffly, noting Alex' lack of response.

"Of course!" he relented. "Thank you so much for all of your help. I'll be in touch. Here's my card. Please, contact me directly if you need anything or have any questions," he said to Tracy while he gathered his baggage, leaving one card by the phone. "And for your help!" waving goodbye. "He looks well." he said to Jennifer, the nurse, over his shoulder as he exited the room. She stood blinking and then turned about to her tend to her patient.

Alex left the infirmary wondering about the implications of this all and the unfortunate morbidity rate. How did they know that no one else was left alive? He wondered. He needed to go see for himself. While en route to his hotel, he uploaded the recording to the cloud, booked a chopper, and emailed Townsend an update. He set down his belongings, washed and shaved his face, ordered a sandwich from room service, and took a taxi to the helipad.

"Alex." he introduced himself to the pilot.

"Cairo." the dark-haired pilot responded. Alex took note of the man's youthful gold-flecked eyes and wondered how old the kid was. "So, you need to fly over the Mariana Trench?" he asked. Alex put on his seat belt and headset so they could communicate over the roar of the blades since the glossy craft had already begun its ascent. He fitted his headset over his ears, adjusted the mouthpiece, tapped it, and then explained what he was hoping to see in better detail.

"Yes, Sir." the pilot acknowledged in compliance. "I hope you're not looking for survivors. I mean, there's not much left out there." Alex nodded, verifying that he'd heard the man but indicated that he needed to decide that for himself. The aircraft sliced through the aerosphere cleanly with ease. "We'll be there in fifteen minutes." Cairo remarked, turning his head in Alex' direction for just a moment and then falling quiet as he meditatively maneuvered the craft. The copter rose and dipped with the grace and agility of a bird of prey, riding the zephyr like a gentle roller coaster.

    As they left the coast, Alex began seeing unidentifiable debris floating. As they flew over the barge, he was shocked to see that it was bobbing not lopsided but entirely upside down. He had been told that under no circumstances that could occur. The force needed to flip a platform of that size did not exist in nature. He instructed the pilot to fly as low as possible, and he examined the charred remains of more than one individual or parts of several people. The cadavers were now very waterlogged, and he suddenly began rethinking shoveling down that meal he'd hastily eaten before he left. He was even more surprised to see the geyser that Tracy had described still flowing only with less force. It was now just bubbling over the area, which must have been where they punctured that cavity in the oceanic base. The pilot drove the scene in circles until he indicated they had burned through their fuel. Alex gave a thumbs up, authorizing a return to shore. As they lifted, he noticed a sheen on the water's surface in an area. Not an oil slick, but something else

"Hey? What is that?" he asked the pilot, pointing.

"I don't know. Fish or something," he replied with zero interest, his goal remaining to return to shore before they ran out of gas. Alex assessed that it was vast as they gained more height, like a big sheet of something. He supposed it was hard to tell how big it was from this height. Maybe 100, maybe 1,000 feet wide. He got out his phone and began filming. Tightening his seatbelt, he leaned over the edge of the copter recording and instructed, "Stay here a minute, nice and low." The pilot rolled his eyes and reread his gauges.

"Yeah, Joe," he obeyed. Alex could only

tell where the thing was on the top of the water, but it looked like it might actually be below the surface level. He could only ever see it when the sun glinted off of it because it was relatively translucent. Maybe it's a type of algae or something, he thought, grasping for any relative concept he was familiar with. He looked around, considering methods to gather more information. The ocean suddenly fell lower and lower beneath them as they rose, rendering anything in the water invisible even to his camera lens. This seemed like what the geologist may have referred to but much more significant. He didn't say it was massive. Alex noticed a pebble on the floorboard of the aircraft.

"Hey, drop as low as you can," he instructed.

"Just for a minute, Man. We're out of time." the pilot informed him.

"Yeah. Fine." He was beyond exhaustion anyway and ready for this workday to be over with. Cairo descended with a frightening speed; Alex was almost free falling. The pilot chortled at the foreigner's obvious discomfort.

"That's as low as I can go. It burns fuel to rise and fall," he said, raising his palms up and down. Nodding, Alex turned back toward the water and hit record again. He dropped the rock, recording the descent as it went hurtling down toward the center of the mass. As the rock drew near, the creature leaped up and grabbed the rock devouring it. It reacted biologically, he surmised, astounded. It seemed to take the form of a more complex animal with jaws or limbs simultaneously and then unassimilating before he could even speak.

CHAPTER TEN

MERMAIDS

HATTIE AND JUSTINE, two young schoolteachers, enjoyed a day out on Grandfather Lyon's sailboat soaking up the last bit of summer on the Pacific Coast. Their kids, aged three, five, and six, ran the deck with the excitement of a summer's day on the gently rocking sea.

"Hadley, get back from that edge!" her mother called, looking over the top of her sunglasses from her sunny spot on the deck, her drink nearly spilling over the edge of her highball.

"Mama, the water is so shiny," Hadley observed. Little Gracie Lane toddled over with big brother Daxon hot on her heels, looking over the edge of the Napa Valley Wildflower, sticking fingers through the lifeline netting installed just for them.

"Stay away from the water, or you guys will have to play inside the cabin," Christine warned from her lounge chair, golden skin glistening with oil, careful not to ding her wet nail polish.

"Yes, Mama." Gracie ceded as the kids ran back to their game of catamaran. The two relaxed as they heard the kids squealing with laughter further from the edge as they gossiped about their awkward principal and her new suspected love interest.

"I mean, I could tell from the day we had that welcome meeting." Hattie explained, swishing around her drink. "I always sensed something funny going on between those two." Chris giggled, enraptured by the excessive leisure of her first summer vacation as a teacher while soaking up the sun with the knowledge that this precious time was all theirs.

"Oooh! Look at this tan line!" Christine announced as she pulled her bathing suit strap off her tawny shoulder."

"Golden Goddess!" Hattie exclaimed seductively, fluttering her eyelashes dramatically and downing the contents of her glass. Giggling, she popped up to pour another, still twittering at her own hilarity.

"What about me?" Christine crooned, standing up, gulping her last sip, and releasing her damp thighs from her sweaty, sun blazon seat. As the ladies headed down the steps for crushed ice and to seek out another bottle, the water nearby glimmered inexplicably.

Dase laid out a little blanket for girls near the stern of the boat. While on suntanned bellies, the two girlies nibbled on cheddar cheese cubes and a bunch of grapes. With mouths full, the children talked theoretically about the sparkling water. Daxon hopped up and ran off.

"The sparkling water is where mermaids come… come to sing songs to real men." Gracie speculated. "Yeah, but, -" she began again, having another thought, "-they are not scary!" she assured her rapt audience with a flourish of chubby fingers.

"Well, I think that the sparkling water…." Hadley supplied, squinting in deep thought.

"What water?" Daxon queried, joining back in after returning from peeing off the port side.

"That glitter water!" Grace pointed just off as he wiped his damp hands on his trunks before diving back into the snacks.

"Well, why is the water so twinkly?" Daxon inquired, splaying his fingers and clasping his fists to illustrate the sparkle, a tiny stream of grape juice emitting from the space where he had a missing front tooth, the new one just budding from his top gum.

"It's 'cause of the mer- mermaids. The fish ..." Hadley's words fell away as she peered at the iridescent sheet caramel tresses blowing over her shoulders in the breeze. While the children chattered, the gelatinous blob stretched out into an extensive sheet, thinning. They fell silent as they observed a seagull land directly onto the mat. It dipped but didn't tear as the bird settled onto it to preen. The hen lifted a wing and tucked her beak underneath, separating her feathers with the ridges in her beak, removing the tough sheathes from her newly molted feathers. She diligently pulled and spat out the debris a few times before tucking her head back under to fluff out her down. As the bird twisted her neck to clean up the feathers on her mantle, Hadley took a step closer to the aft, curiously noticing one area of the aqueous carpet creeping up in a silent wave. Eyes widening, she saw that the glimmering sheet had suddenly begun to gather more density. Suddenly uneasy and unable to speak. She reached out for Daxon, keeping her eyes fixed on the creature. He was still sitting, asking his sister about her fish people. Stretching, Hadley found his forearm and, speechless, tugged.

Gracie and Daxon both turned to look out at the water. The shimmering blanket suddenly became wildly predacious. The flat film suddenly took rigid form the shape of razor-toothed, voracious jaws, folding that bird in half in one bone-breaking crunch and pulling her under the sea before she could struggle or release any more than a gargled call of alarm. A single down feather was left floating in the air where she had been. The children peered, frozen, leaning over the railing while the cocoon, just under the water's surface, appeared to be masticating the still living fowl, blood spurts emanating from the broil. Baffled sounds of struggle, oxygen bubbles, and gore escaped the chrysalis, seeping into the ocean water. Meal devoured; the gelatinous creature resumed its unassuming glassy, flat form only detectable by the sheen cast on the water's surface.

"Mom! Mommy! Mama!" The children ran shrieking for their mothers, tumbling down the steps into the safety of the cabin, attempting to relay the horrifying tale killing the women's buzz in an instant. Dason's lime green sunglasses, which had fallen from his sweaty brow, dropped in the water. They floated slowly down a transitory depth, surrounded by a milky cloud released by the blob. The glasses were quickly engulfed and combined with the surrounding lifeforms and minerals to form a significant mass that swiftly sank into the deep dark depths evacuated from the sea.

CHAPTER ELEVEN

HOOFSTOCK

IT WAS A BLISTERING morning in Fairfield, North Dakota. John watched the sun creep over the horizon from his vantage point on the front deck, lighting the landscape. He sipped his steaming cup of obsidian, his lips pursing slightly after each bitter sip as was his Saturday ritual. Coffee down, he walked out to the feed barn to care for livestock. Hearing the grasshoppers collide with denim overalls, he rustled through the wild wheatgrass and clover. The tall man with a powerful build watched the flying insect life begin to animate as they worked their way over the flowers and native grasses crawling and buzzing about. He thought about what the neighbor said about all the lakes being higher than they'd ever been in recorded history and became lost in preponderance.

He was rugged and wild. His slightly shaggy hair fell into his hazel eyes as he leaned down into the feed bags. He scooped out swine pellet and pulled off six flakes of alfalfa and half a Folgers tin of sweet feed. The muscles in his back flexed as he stood with nearly half a bale of hay on his shoulder and the few canisters of meal hanging in beat-up buckets in calloused hands. He squinted as some dust and debris from the grass wafted around him, his mind still elsewhere. Noisy oinks and slurps roused him back to his chores. He stopped, beaming at the ripe spotted sow and ravenous piglets, eleven in this litter. He thought back to when mother pig was a greedy little piglet herself. She had come to them as an orphan. Josie and Nicolas had bottle-fed her day and night. That piglet screamed her head off when ready for that tit. Chuckling at that memory, he tossed the swine fodder into the stall.

Sarah, the robust dappled sow, and her piglets rooted and snorted in delight at the delivery. He leaned over the splintered goat pen to drop in the hay and a pinch of grain. Next, he entered the horse barn where Hondo, the Mustang, Buttermilk the creamy Welsh Pony, and Beau the old bay thoroughbred stood waiting quietly for their breakfasts. Hondo approached the feeder, swatting at the mosquitoes with his tail. Buttermilk whinnied in excitement, and Beau snickered quietly. The man put his large, warm hands on the face of the bay, his old friend. He looked deeply into the large round eyes of this animal, and they looked back into his, almond irises reading into the depths of the farmer's sepia gaze.

"I know," John said aloud, firmly patting the horse's muscular neck. "Nic will be back soon, and then he'll be feeding you again. And you just want food, don't you?" the man acknowledged, chortling, realizing that, really, he was talking to himself. The giant horse nickered again, seeming to understand. He picked up three flakes of hay and dumped the sweet-smelling grain into the big horse's trough. He gave the mustang two flakes, and pony got one, to which they each got to work quickly. He reached out for the pony's neck. Little Buttermilk had been his son's barrel horse when he was little, although he'd outgrown him. Besides, the boy didn't have much time for riding or spending time with the livestock these days. Like all the teens in the area, he planned his thrilling escape from Bumfuck, Nowhere. His dad understood. He knew his son wanted to see the world. And so, with his Christmas bonus, he bought two tickets for a Caribbean cruise for his wife and son.

"He's seventeen now. We don't have much more time with him before he leaves, and if we end on a low note, he may not come back here to visit his folks once he's gone," his wife fretted. They were good, salt-of-the-earth people who loved their son. This seemed like a sad truth. So, for Christmas, the family present was for the two to go on a cruise the following summer; that was a gift he was really excited about. He couldn't believe that his best friend couldn't go, but his dad told him he could make new friends on the ship. It would be for seven days. Maybe he'd even meet a girl, he proffered.

After battling the barrage of crickets on the way back to the house, John sat at his computer to check his email. He had a notification that his cloud had been filled to capacity. He wondered how that could be when he'd just upgraded their package unless someone had dumped their entire device. That had happened the last time Nic switched cell phones. He opened it and, surprised, began perusing the photos and videos from the cruise. Pictures of Nickie and Josie in the restaurant dining on exotic seafood. Nicolas climbing a rock wall. A short video of him swimming and Josie lying in a lounge chair in her bathing suit with her hair in curlers. She said she planned to see a magic show that first night but the kid didn't want to go. He'd rather stay by the pool, he said. After that, he smiled at the various selfies that each was taking of themselves. A photo of Josie by herself in a casino, Nic eating hot wings with a group of boys around his age. Nic and a girl on the upper deck watching the sunset, his arm slung comfortably over her shoulder. The ocean seemed to go on forever. Then there was another video. Nicolas was on the ship's prow with another girl pointing out the massive wake the watercraft left behind. Some little kids were horsing around nearby. The girl left his side to go join her family.

"Hey, but what's your name? I'm Nic!" he called after her. His dad chuckled at his son's tenacity. The camera panned out to the water, where the wildlife was putting on a show. He heard some passengers talking about dolphins, but as Nic's camera zoomed in, John could see that those were whales jumping out of the water. Maybe, blue whales leaping frantically. With the phone's focal eye honing in better than the human eye, the camera lens could see a massive beast in pursuit of them. The colossus broke the water's surface, jaws gaping with an inconceivable jaw of razors. In a breathtaking spiral, following the arc of the whales, jaws gaping, she clamped down the back two-thirds half of a whale with incredible bear trap-like force and landed artfully back into the ocean with almost no splash. John rubbed his eyes and refocused on the footage. There was an eerie silence as the ship's passengers hung over the railing, frozen.

The water around the area was quickly ensanguined as the sapphire water turned purple with lifeblood. So much blood. The scene had unfolded a few hundred feet from the ship. As people began to look at each other in terror. A colossal fin broke the water approaching the bow and then resubmerged. The center of the ship made a loud cracking sound. The impact of the blow knocked passengers off their feet. Screaming and cries erupted as vacationers ran, seeking the safety of their loved ones. Others fell to their feet, clinging to the railing. A few dove for shelter.

The ship split down the center, with the

fault line crawling up the vessel's keel. The weight shifted, knocking people further off balance. The pound of gushing water instantaneously filled their ears as they began taking on water. Frantic shrieking escalated as the spray rocketed up toward them. The crack in the hull snapped and echoed loudly. The ship broke into two, attached loosely by a thin bandage of metal, the two ends quickly becoming waterlogged in the center, causing the ship's ends to slowly stand upright. People hung on for dear life, murmuring prayers and pleas for redemption. John watched the scene unfold in horror, knowing he would never see this wife and child again. His fists clenched and released as he considered that he had sent his family off to suffer this death sentence by buying them those tickets against his better judgment, but they'd desperately wanted to go.

As he waited for them to slowly sink into the waters, the death machine lurking, a colossal shadow loomed in the depths. Suddenly, it burst from the ocean like a torpedo. Spinning up and over the ship, tail oscillating as if she were swimming through the air. She landed aboard with the force of an earthquake, causing water lines onboard to rupture, geyser erupting from the terrace. Onlookers watching the scene unfold in astonishment. She snapped the observation deck as she thrashed, obliterating wood, metal, and flesh in her path. With one flip of her tail, she smashed the visitor's information center, sending mangled passengers sprawling into the sea. She writhed, looking at the ship's bow with one enormous glacial eye!

Her thick cartilaginous sclera intelligently darted the rods and cones: seeking. With one powerful wave of her body, she collapsed the top deck crushing those praying for refuge below. Screams erupted, and fires ignited from the engine room as the craft suddenly began to take on more water. Those still watching were perplexed by the fact that this shark no longer appeared the slate gray that she first appeared to be but more of the teak color of the deck, and on this 1200-foot ship, she seemed to take up over half the vessel. This wasn't possible, of course, but there she was. She began to convulse wildly, collapsing levels upon levels of the ship as she sunk, finally shattering the craft into countless pieces and plummeting violently back into the swell, the death toll rising with each whip of her tail.

Suddenly, Nicolas' camera went overboard. In the last seconds of the footage, his father could hear him sobbing loudly. The camera plummeted downward, submerged, and bubbles trailed skyward before the footage went black. This was the end.

John sat on his gingham couch motionless, unable to speak, think, or process any part of what he just saw. Outside, the world continued to turn. The birdsong went on. The breeze tussled the wildflowers. A large sapphire, ruby-eyed dragonfly settled the on the screen door, resting up for his afternoon mosquito hunt, peering into the house curiously and observing the enormous man as he wept.

CHAPTER TWELVE

NO TOUCHY

Two Weeks Later

UNBELIEVABLY, ANTON WAS chiding himself for his ultimate lack of resolve in offering Rukia snacks. Smiling proudly at his strange little dog perched happily on the office chair next to him, he decided he had made the right choice to accept this job. His was hired as the chief cyber data analysis for the Pentagon. Well, really it was this or incarceration but this was working out just fine. Especially, when Rukia looked at him with those runny little eyes. She had her pup tent on the cushy chair to his left so he could pet her and offer treats while still keeping one hand flying across the keyboard.

He now had a big corner office next door to the boundless processors he had ordered. Mysteriously, this half-million dollars in equipment had been billed to the jerk who made him eat pavement when he was taken into custody. Anton now had an enormous glass desk with a dozen monitors and split screens from which to view several feeds simultaneously. Ten o clock, he noted. With the click of one button, all screens became one. Time to Netflix and lunch. It was true, he took an early lunch but he worked best in spurts. The truth was that he took a second lunch at 1:00 and then took Rukia for a walk at 2:30 and often didn't return to the office until the next day. That was until he got into a flow. Then sometimes he would work without coming up for air for 36 hours straight. Given the freedom to work however suited him, he actually liked this job. And the salary! Wow! There were a lot of zeros in that salary! The best perk, besides being allowed is canine companion, was immunity from any law that he may or may not have broken in the past, present, or future due to the fine print he included in the hacked version of his contract. He could work remotely if he chose, but at this point, why would he? The subsequent demand he made was that he be segregated from all of his colleagues except for one. No one else was permitted to interact with him. He had no dress code and zero obligation to socialize. Furthermore, he could make his hours. He had a fridge in his office, his own water cooler, and all the processing power of which a boy could dream.

He was given a personal assistant who was an MIT graduate still in her 20s. He liked her. Her name was short and no nonsense: Dru. She was very pretty, large doll-like eyes, about 5'6 with curly hair and impeccably dressed but Anton was oblivious to all of that. Her assistant was an AI named FROLO. She had told him what that acronym stood for but, not caring, he discarded that information immediately. Anton liked FROLO because he didn't talk or have eyes that you had to look at like people wanted you to do. He was essentially a skeletal frame with a number of tools. The robot reminded Anton of a Swiss army knife that could do math and deliver snacks. FROLO was good and Dru wasn't bad herself. She could read a room and, for the most part, Anton didn't notice whether she was there or not. When he needed something, she would bring it. Basically, she understood him well enough to not interrupt his process. Little did he notice, she kept regular office hours and, for the most part, worked alongside him running algorithms from a small desk on the other side of the room. She even had her own formula to determine when he might need a break or food. Her predictions were about ninety-five percent accurate after day five. She made him a digital choice board to offer him break and snack suggestions warding off decision fatigue. Her system was working beautifully.

After he came in six days in a row, in the same stretched out clothes, she ordered him replicas of the same worn-out t-shirt and sweatpants. She had them laundered and prepared for him to change into when he arrived but he touched them once and said those new clothes made his hair tickle. That concept she didn't follow but she respected it nonetheless. She nearly giggled aloud when he finally tried them. He dropped his drawers right in front of her, bum exposed, no underwear. Tittering, she turned away and went back into her corner office to give him some privacy. She sent FROLO to retrieved the dirty ones so they could be washed and returned. Her feelings of delighted victory soon changed when she saw that his lack of productivity decreased by 80 percent and the next two days were overrun with excessive coughing and throat clearing throughout the day which she documented were some of tics indicating elevated stress levels. It's a no wonder he looks the way he does, she lamented, feeling a bit guilty for judging him.

This kid was a savant whose abilities surpassed his superior's understanding. Odd though he may be, he wasn't unhinged. Carefully raised by loving parents who sheltered him and reared him in understanding kindness, he had remained unbelievably humble. He never let the power go to his head and upheld a strict moral code. He occasionally harnessed that energy to his behest, but it was all harmless.

Besides being slightly dog-obsessed and socially awkward, he was pretty balanced. More importantly, he could decipher codes at a glance with help from his eidetic memory, but he still had rational understanding, unlike most people who were cursed or blessed with his gifts. He was an astounding statistician and had an uncanny ability to connect unrelated facts and puzzle pieces to gain insight. With unlimited resources, it did not take him long to piece together the big picture of what was occurring on a global scale. With access to all information from the internet, radio, phones, CCTV, security footage, drones, and satellite, he worked on something vital. Something that may just be causing the end of everything as humans know the world, anyway.

      He had been employed to solve a problem. He had been informed of a potential pandemic, a failed accident on the government's behalf; this virus was only supposed to get out just before the election. It was supposed to stay controlled, only exposing tiny pockets of the population to frighten the public into action. Well, that didn't go so well. So, Plan B was to blame the Chinese wet food market. Blaming the Chinese? How trite, he thought, considering himself being half-Chinese. Now, his job was to track down a scientist who could develop a cure or at least a vaccine and redirect the media after the election.

Once he had been given the actual data regarding the "crisis," he was unphased, knowing this rouge virus was a less potent killer than Influenza B or H1N1, which the human race had survived without too much suffering. He waited a reasonable amount of time and then suggested a few recipes for vaccines. He had hacked one voice mail from the scientist who secretly took credit for accidentally releasing the virus after downing an 18 pack of beer while working late on Christmas Eve in Seattle. He was going to push that they name it something in a personal reference to that. Suffering had ensued, but too many people were on this crazy rock anyway. I mean, that is nature's way. People were science's bitch. There was no way around it, is what he thought about it.

However, since being given metaphorical keys to the castle, he followed a lead he'd been working on. A few things he'd seen had raised the hackles on Rukia's back when he told her of what he'd suspected. Of course, Rukia's hackles were only raised because she was stretching, but this is how Anton worked through larger-than-life problems. His first task was to gather data, categorize the information, and formulate a rating system for potential danger. The risk categories ranged from one to ten, with ten being world-ending. World governments spy through all tech. There's no 6-9 in Anton's system as there was no need, and he was not a guy who wasted time, at least not in his mind. There were some things that he had seen from a pinpoint perspective. However, with his new level of omniscience, he had pieced together a reel of footage: sat footage of the decimation of a Philippine whaler's ship, a hilarious Snapchat posted by a college professor, the private diary of a manager of a PR firm for some oil tycoon, a looney epileptic priest, some raving native on a street corner talking about the ocean coming to get us or something... and then there was the disappearance of an entire cruise ship all of which seemed to be tied up somehow. He could see a pattern, a chain of cause-and-effect, even if he hadn't put his finger on exactly how, but he calculated that it was escalating into something groundbreaking and not in a good way. What to do? He pondered silently. He tilted his head and blinked in the form to signal his earpiece to dial phone extension #139.

"Michaels, I'm going to need a team."

CHAPTER THIRTEEN

HOLY TRIN

FATHER CHRISTOPHER JOHNSON ended his call with the Holy Trinity Roman Catholic Church Monsignor on 42nd St in New York City. They'd discussed the Celebration of the Ascension of the Lord and the issue of the dwindling congregation. The clergy was under pressure from the Archdiocese to grow, but despite attempts, people weren't coming. As the assistant priest, he was tasked with the dreadful job of recruiting new members. Additionally, he acted as the Executive Administrator for Academic Affairs New York Theological Seminary, which kept him busy.

Despite his focused apostolic pursuits, he'd felt spiritually isolated of late.

Each vicar was assigned different jobs, and duties had been piling up as members of the priesthood continued to fall away. Father Dudley died unexpectedly from premature heart failure at age 37. Father Thomas had chosen to leave the Catholic church and become a pastor so he could marry. Father Roman, who was 96, passed away in his sleep, although he had not been very strong in the area of service over the last several years. For the last few years, Christopher has been enduring a crisis of faith, a disconcerting separation from God. Throughout his lifetime, he had spent time worldwide bringing people hope through their walk with God. Seeing the miracle of salvation amidst squalor rejuvenated his faith in his youth. He considered it was time to travel abroad again, but he thought not. Already in his late fifties, he was overweight and less energetic than his past self. The memory of trudging through the swamps in Hati made him break out into a sweat.

He had been lacking the divine inspiration he experienced in his youth. As a consequence, he began to question his purpose in the church. For the last month or two, he'd been plagued with blinding migraines that debilitated him; they started with tingling numbness in his right hand and an acrid taste on his tongue. Those were signs of the pain to come. Grimacing now at the taste, nervously flexing his hands open and closed, he retrieved his satchel, thumping off the light switch, retiring early for the day. It was already after four, and he knew he wouldn't be able to function fifteen minutes from now. Reluctantly, he decided that he had better get to walking. Taking some deep breaths, he did his best to remain calm. His goal was to make it into his apartment in the clergy house without making it apparent that he was in distress.

Heading down the path and shortcutting through the grass, he fumbled in his pockets for the old brass key. As he neared the rectory door, he saw stars as the blinding pain amplified. Usually, he relished this walk as he traversed the parish campus, enjoying the historical architecture of the ancient buildings contrasting the bustling sharp lines and modernity of downtown. He enjoyed the beauty of the climbing vines and the chirping sparrows making sport in the birdbaths. He appreciated the carefully sculpted gardens, but not today. Huffing, he closed the door. Hastily, he dropped his bag on the floor, kicked off his shoes, and fumbled toward his cot just as an ice pick hammered his crown, knees buckling, the content of his stomach roiled. He grappled for the metal frame of his bed and heaved himself up, finding a brief modicum of strength, knowing he could be incapacitated for hours. He closed his eyes, focused on his breathing, and, a moment later, began to convulse.

Sometimes, well after dark, he was roused slowly by the quiet chatter of two concerned voices. Rolling over, he felt a damp towel fall away from his face, causing the bright light of the harsh overhead lighting to blind him momentarily. Detecting a remnant flavor of stomach acid in the back of his throat and the crust of vomit on his neck, he smacked his lips, his mouth tasting sour. He reached for the towel, wiped his face and neck with the towel, and cautiously pushed himself up to sit. Blinking, the two men became silent, observing Christopher rise. Quieting, they stood in tandem approaching him with reserve.

"Christopher?" the Monsignor began. "Are you well?" he asked slowly. Dazed and weakened but no longer under duress, he was perplexed as to why an audience was in his apartment supervising him. Wiping his eyes, he noticed the sun coming in from the west window. The Monsignor continued, "Father Belli, overheard you... uh... yelling and thought you were being attacked. He used the master keys to enter and was surprised to find you in some catatonic state, alone. He called me. We tried to wake you, and when we did, you sat up and began babbling. God's truth, Christopher, we first feared possession. Having your fit behind us, we agree that it seemed like more of a hallucinogenic state of delirium brought on by fever."

"Fever?" Christopher questioned in complete confusion.

"Well, there was no fever, per se, but a sickness. We video-recorded the episode. Father Belli said that he's suspecting something amiss for a little while. He came to me two weeks ago, and I asked him to keep an eye on you. He already had permission to enter your suite when you didn't answer him from the door."

The ailing man's gaze traveled from one trusted friend to the other.

"Thank you, but I... I think I just need rest." He waved his hand, flicking fingers up in a gentle conveyance to excuse his guests for the evening.

"No." The Monsignor insisted. "Christopher, take a look."

The priest walked, tottering, to the empty seat at his tiny kitchenette, where a hot cup of tea sat at the meager table. The phone, propped up on a canister of sugar, began to play a 2-minute video of him sitting, stiff as a board with his eyes opened disturbingly wide, raving like a lunatic about something difficult to decipher. He seemed to be sharing the perspective of some intelligent beast in the sea.

From what they could interpret, he saw through the eyes of a marine animal. How remained a mystery.

He rambled about how She, the immortal, is empathetic and seeking lifeforms. In the beginning, she was just a baby, reborn upon explosion released from her tomb. She emerged from the nest and instinctively began establishing her territory, floating and feeding. Swimming, growing, feeding, devouring, her form evolving as she developed. Mother Earth was calling to her. No, to them, a whole fleet of them. Calling them to work. As they nursed and matured, they altered the sea through their life cycle.

Christopher apparently saw all this unfolding from the consciousness of a massive shark-like endoskeleton. A form unlike that of any modern-day shark. It was so strong that it protected these animals from being crushed in the depths like a submarine, granting them a massive range. What will happen to the land when most of the fish are gone? He felt her wonder as she traveled, insatiable and driven. While in his fugue, he felt primal, ancient, only driven by instinct; his only clear conscious understanding was that Mother was hurting. Chris squinted, studying the footage as the fit seemed to abate.

"Mother is hurting. Mother is hurting. Mother... Yes. Mother..." speechless, he watched himself, babbling until his tensed body became lax, and he fell into a resting state that appeared like a dreamless sleep.

"Christopher, you slept for many hours, unresponsive until you rolled over and regurgitated." His superior informed in concern.

"What is this all about?" Father Belli queried. "Have you been watching those scientific theory shows again? We called the rectory physician, and he explained that this appeared to be a seizure, but he said this was unlike most. He said that you may have developed epilepsy. Stress can cause uncontrolled bursts of electrical energy in the brain's nerve cells that alter awareness. They can result in convulsions or affect our senses and emotions. He said this appeared to be a tonic-clonic seizure." While listening to this seeming admonishment, he wiped at his streaming eyes in embarrassment. The Monsignor tenderly laid a damp, cool towel on his brow, unease shimmering in his eyes.

"Since you'd come in early and laid down, he said that this was likely not your first and that you were already familiar with the aura that overcomes an individual before a seizure. Most unusual was that most people experience confusion regarding their own experiences, not something manifested." He droned on. Chris was no longer listening. The Monsignor moved close to the man, who was like a son putting one clammy hand on his protégé's shoulder.

"Christopher, why hadn't you come to me if you were sick?" The priest sat without answers for the two men with looks of grave concern. Before this, he hadn't recollection of the experience afterward, only the sallow afterglow of an overwhelming ominous feeling. Now that he'd heard his own ravings, he recalled some of the visions firsthand. He knew one thing that they had not yet gleaned. This world of theirs may be coming to an end soon. He wondered if this was the end of days dreading that he saw may be real and not an electrical manifestation of an epileptic brain. Why he thought this, he couldn't say. At a loss for words, he said nothing. Seeing he needed rest, the Monsignor consoled him.

"Well, Son, you seem well enough for now. I'm putting you on a sabbatical for three days. You have an appointment for some testing at the hospital on Wednesday. We'll meet again after we get your results. Don't worry about anything for now. Just rest. Call Father Belli if you need anything. We'll take over your duties for now." He clapped his hand on the man's chest, looking him in the eye, but Chris remained despondent. He mustered a weak smile that emboldened the two men to trust that it was safe for them to take their leave. He nodded acknowledgment and mumbled thanks as they left, locking his front door behind them.

Momentarily, Chris stood, stripped out of his uniform, and went to take a shower. When the water turned warm, he stepped under the stream. As the water pelted him, he had sudden hair-raising flashbacks of his vision. He was... She: ravenous, powerful, searching, destroying our world one menacing mouthful at a time. He could feel her gaining strength, perilously knowledgeable of the plan, cognizant this was not her first existence and would not be her last. His head sagged as the searing water fell upon him, exhausted but rationalizing that this vision must not have been accurate. He was sick, and the doctors would figure it out soon enough. Holding onto that thought, he gave the tension in his muscles permission to ebb. He bathed until the water became arctic and then made himself a meager meal of Apple Cinnamon Instant Quaker Oats before turning out the light and sleeping like the dead.

CHAPTER FOURTEEN

UNEXPECTED COMPANY

"HURRY UP, YOU!" Evelyn said, rapping a friendly reminder on the bathroom door after noticing the pinging of the shower water still running.

"I have an eight o'clock class on Tuesdays!" she smiled, reminding him, intoxication over their reunion still absurdly apparent. She buttoned her blouse below her collarbone over a pale pink lace chemise plucking modest diamond studs from her jewelry box. Fitting them into her ears intuitively, she gazed out the panoramic windows from their bedroom loft, appreciating the wash of color, sun peeking through the trees. Gliding over to the armoire, she selected a vibrant scarlet blazer pulling it on over her stoic, white blouse, tailored to hug her petite but curvy frame. She slipped slender feet into dainty a pair of kitten heels, feminine but still reasonable for traversing the expansive campus in a bustling fashion, nodding in satisfaction, when she heard the tell-tale squeak of the shower knobs turning off. She chuckled, hearing the damp towel snap in protest yanked from the railing on the wall. She had to cover her mouth to keep from laughing aloud, listening to Adem groan loudly as he always did during his I-hate-mornings ritual. She glanced in the vanity mirror, artfully sweeping her hair up into a massive French twist-bun at her crown and securing it with two tortoiseshell hair sticks, pulling loose the few tendrils that weren't entirely caught in the twist, falling they framed her face. She smiled reticently, noticing how this classic style highlighted her distinctive mixed ethnic features, which she knew he especially appreciated. She glanced at her watch, prepared to knock again to offer the current time along with her prediction of the traffic report.

She paused to listen when she heard Kanik barking, Stranger here. She marched toward the sliding glass doors on the balcony, taking in the overhead view of three black SUVs out front with two suited men exiting from the first vehicle. She watched curiously, her brow furrowing with mild alarm. She called for Adem when she saw an armed man and woman with earpieces get out of the second vehicle eying at Kanik taking stock of the perimeter. The first two mounted the stairs and began to approach the front door. The third pair looked as if they were going around back. As the wolf-dog heightened the alarm, the second car's driver made some hand signal to the passenger of the third vehicle. They were signaling to assist the second car, who approached looking from the high ground nearest the garage. Distracted by the gunmen, she was startled when warm water droplets dripped down her temple as a naked Adem towered over her, damping the back of her jacket and peering over her shoulder.

"They look like government goons," he noted, perturbed as he stretched his undershirt across his chest and then over his head. Grabbing his work shirt, he swirled it behind him like a cape pulling his arms in, left then right, as he descended the stairs barefooted to answer the knock at the kitchen door, shirt unbuttoned. Staying just on his heels, Evie followed, increasingly intrigued by what they could want.

As he pulled open the door, the apparent lead man pulled off his sunglasses and manifested a federal badge. "Doctor Adem James Humboldt and Doctor Evelyn Marie Humboldt?" he inquired, blazing blue eyes without any humor.

"Yes?" they replied in unison. He went on.

"I am Special Agent Clark with the U.S. Department of Interior, Bureau of Safety of Environmental Special Circumstances. Special Agent Wager here is an Intelligence Analyst with the Federal Bureau of Investigation." The slender agent with a gun on her hip nodded in agreement. Her hazel eyes narrowed as she took stock of the couple, jaw jutting in intensity. "We have assembled a team, and you both need to come with us. It is an urgent matter of national security, which is all we can tell you at this time. You'll be more thoroughly debriefed when we reach our rendezvous."

"There is a chopper waiting at the top of the hill. We've already informed the University of Berkeley of your impending absence," she added, and he nodded matter-of-factly, first to Adem and then to Evelyn. Agent Wager took a few steps back, putting her sunglasses back on, and concluding this declaration. When the two remained unmoving, Agent Clark said, "We'll wait."

He nodded respectfully, giving the doctors a moment to digest this information. Agent Wager conversed quietly with her double, allowing a few feet of privacy. He nodded and signaled something to the agents who waited below. The scientists stared at each other.

"Wait for what?" she leaned out, asking incredulously.

"Ma'am. You can't bring your dog, and you might want to pack a bag." Agent Wager instructed the bewildered pair on what must be done next.

"I'll call Doc Smith to see if he has room in the clinic for a border. Pup needs his medicine." Adem said to his wife. Warmly, she put a hand on his shoulder in gratitude.

"I'm going to pack us a bag," she stated

in reciprocity, her body turning obediently, but her mind was racing. Fifteen minutes later, they were given earmuffs and boarded an aircraft already primed for takeoff. One very concerned dog clearly objecting to this avian swallowing his parents and flying them into the sky.

They began to rise from the Earth before their restraint had even been fastened. In an instant, Evelyn could see an aerial view of their house, neighborhood, city, county, then... clouds. They made the five-hour flight in two hours and forty-five minutes, a loud and tumultuous ride. Their legs felt gelatinous when they landed and disembarked, ringing in their ears. Endorphins began to course through their veins, quickly making things feel serious. They approached the Pentagon and were swiftly ushered into the National Military Command Center, a room inaccessible to the public. The gravity of what must be occurring began to set in.

CHAPTER FIFTEEN

CADRE

"DOCTORS, MEET THE Team." Their crisply dressed escort broadcast as the couple was escorted to a table with other bewildered-looking men and women and one kid. "I am Michaels, the Pentagon's Director of International Crisis Resolution." "Everyone, these are Doctor and Doctor Humboldt, the lead scientific investigators." He said to the group. Pointing to a strikingly handsome Filipino in his late 20s, "This is Tracy John, the geologist present at what we now believe to be Exposure One." Turning his gaze to the delicate-boned young woman dressed in a smart suit, he pointed, "This is Emmie Longoria. She's a doctoral student in informational sciences whose existing Ph. D. is in Media Research and Journalism. She has experience in the data collection process of investigations of this nature. Alexander Becker, CEO of Quality Control Safety and Environmental Manager of Dominion Petroleum Corporation, seems responsible for the initiation of release of the creatures, and up front is Anton Isaac. He's our Cyber Data Analyst and Statistician. Though he is the youngest team member, he is also the coordinator and leader." Someone who could pass for a 15-year-old broke his gaze from some trance when he appeared to change a setting on his glasses. He stifled a snicker, indicating that he was somehow engaged with something humorous. He seemed to mentally disengage and wiped his nose sniffing.

"Sorry. -replay of," he chortled. "Never mind! I'm here." He said, standing and waving one hand in a mock salute. "So, the researchers have arrived." He announced in a neutral tone to no one in particular. "Finally!" he muttered to himself. "I do believe that's everyone!" He proclaimed officially. "Alright!" he said, clapping. "Let's get started." He said, taking his feet off of the glass table.

He rose, his demeanor changing slightly to assume a mild stance of authority. "Long story short, our nation's surveillance system of the public has an informational warning system. The scale rates the following: 1 – 5 normal chatter. 1. How was your day 2.

Strife-related discussion 3. randomly discuss explosions, bombings, murder, 4. organized plans for violence but lack of ability 5. organized intent for school shootings, urban bombings, Unabomber, 9-11, and then there's 10. which is reserved for World War 4, Nuclear War or other world-ending events." He explained nonchalantly. "Yes." He confirmed, meeting the gaze of his bewildered audience. "Our government spies on all of us through any and all technology. Good people, right now, we are at a Ten." He paused, priming himself to untangle the cyber web of a lifetime. He took a deep breath before this hand-chosen group of intellects, examining each individually. "To bring you up to speed-" He broke his train of thought. His mood visibly lightened, "Actually, let's start with lunch!" he decided, changing tactics. "It's going to be a long day!"

After placing a group order from his favorite new hole-in-the-wall in DC, El Rinconcito Café, the questions began to come from various group members. Anton refused to entertain their inquiry and insisted they hold their questions until after his presentation. Only after lunch had been ordered did he present a horrifying video montage that summed up everything he'd decided was related to the current crisis, which he enjoyed referring to as the Cataclysmic Megalodon Calamity or the CMC.

While the smartly dressed, caramel-skinned assistant, Dru, unpacked their lunches, Anton began to unravel what he now knew from the bits of information his algorithm brought to his attention. He explained that the whole sequence started with the explosion on the rig. He pulled up satellite footage and encrypted footage that belonged to Dominion Petroleum. He narrated what was unfolding as he displayed the images on several monitors to establish a comprehensive overview.

"When the riggers breached that cavern, it punctured a hole in a pressurized cabin which released with such force that it caused an explosion of sorts. Theoretically, this pocket was created by the molten igneous rock that cooled too quickly and formed a pocket of oil and gas. Due to the high pressure of the vacuum, it was believed that retrieving it would take less energy. That was, in theory, as no one had previously harvested oil from so deeply under the sea. When the drillers breached the cabin, it punctured a hole in a pressurized cabin that released a geyser of water with such force that it caused an aquatic explosion. TJ was blown clear of the main region of destruction in his boat, which floated adrift." Turning and finding eye contact with the geologist, and asked, "Is it okay if I call you TJ?" without waiting for an answer, he went on. "I just like TJ. So, luckily, TJ, it was fitted with a beacon device which is how you were discovered drifting unconsciously in your boat" He broke his gaze with the geologist and then said to them all. "He was the lone survivor from the crew on that rig. As the geyser finally lost force, a nasty gooey substance was observed on the water's surface.

He next retrieved and projected the

cell phone footage filmed by Becker, demonstrating that the masses had emerged from the cavern, grown and expanded. They had assumed some form and were in three distinct clusters floating on the water's surface that, from a close-up angle, appeared to be aggressively absorbing phytoplankton. This, he surmised, was the embryonic form of the creature. He then pulled up the comical Snapchat footage of Hank and the good doctor. As soon as it was pulled up, Evelyn had her head in her hands and mumbled something. She was given a supportive squeeze on her wrist by her mate.

"I knew it." She whispered to Adem, thinking about the talking she would give sweet Hank if she was ever permitted to return to regular life, which she was beginning to question. His theory was the jellyfish-type animal was the fetal form of the same creature. Emmie covered her mouth in disbelief and amusement at the doctor seeing this clip.

Next, he pulled up some video recordings of a priest having some fit in which he was croaking unintelligibly. He was foaming at the mouth and convulsing when suddenly he sat up wide-eyed and began reciting some kind of deep-sea experience from a first-hand perspective of some monster. The most exciting element of this account was him clearly explicating this innate understanding of this animal, who seemed aware of her surroundings and even had a subconscious knowledge of what may come. From what they could interpret, he had the omniscience on the beast. She was released from the cavern by Dominion. Man released the beasts, but nature stimulated their metamorphosis, birthing them again, as they did many eons ago.

Anton pulled up the following clip without any transition, a YouTube video posted by Donut Diggler Kid entitled 'crasey indiun n my street .' The shaky footage portrayed a young, dark-haired man sitting on a street corner as passersby left small bills, change, and various items at his feet. Initially, he appeared to begin meditatively chanting. This devolved into him pleading with the people of his city about a crisis that no one understood. Compassion for a man who seemed down on his luck seemed to compel a few of them to offer their own alms to this spiritual envoy.

-In the past, my elders have foretold crises such as Small Pox, the Long Walk, and now a new virus. We must renounce our greed and do the ghost dance once again. We must call on the favor of our spirit guides and grieve now for the Pretty Princess. She and her people have been lost and can never be recovered. She will not fall alone, my brothers and sister. We shall all turn to ash together.

"His mention of The Pretty Princess seemed out of place with his cultural background. My algorithms matched this mention to the footage from the Bonnie Baroness, the cruise ship lost at sea. The cruise line was still investigating the events, but I unearthed multiple cell phone videos. This one was in the Google Cloud of

HappyFeet2012. The video was filmed by a child named Paulina and two older girls calling them Thalia and Wednesday. They seemed to be acting out some scenario from the ship's bow. Their presenter paused the footage to explain his conclusion for showing them the next piece. They were laughing and joking when they decided to go find some lunch. At this time, they were suddenly tossed askew. They lost their footing, and the shot jostled as towels and other personal items rolled across the deck. The phone too fell but was caught by the lanyard of the owner's neck. People mumbled and called from their companions as they found their balance. Suddenly, one woman began to shriek.

"Paulina!" one of the girls clamored. She panned toward her sister and then to the water where she was pointing.

"Dolphins! They jump out of the water!" Paulina cried out in excitement.

"Happy Feet," corrected the voice of a woman off-camera, "Those are whales." As the massive ship rocked and bobbed again, you could hear commotion rise, sending the passengers off balance. The fin of the incubus broke the water's surface behind the pod of violently leaping whales near the ship, causing water displacement that made the colossal ship bobble from east to west like a rowboat.

"I'm going to TikTok -" A child's voice trailed off as the footage ended abruptly. After that clip, the lights in the room rose from a dim beam to full strength illuminating Anton in complete seriousness. He took a deep breath and began.

"So, there was no TikTok which indicated that things got calamitous real quick!" he explained, "and we have some random boat anchor with some weird DNA for you science people to check out. It was retrieved off the coast of the Philippines. The ship's remains were from a ship with a history of illegal whaling. The metal was tested for whale DNA so they could take possession of the remains to hold the company liable. The Coast Guard's findings were inconclusive. Two days ago, we had it delivered it here, which is why you two are here." he gestured to Dr. Humboldts. "Well, plus that baby you already caught and was playing with at your school. It arrived here before you landed." Evelyn turned to Adem blinking. Turning to address the whole room, "Questions?" he asked of the entire group, and everyone began talking at once.

"This is about the turd." Adem leaned over and whispered to his wife. She stood rigid in disbelief.

CHAPTER SIXTEEN

CARIBOU COFFEE

AFTER ANSWERING A battery of questions, Anton handed the inquisition over to Dru. Feeling like he had already responded to the most critical questions, Anton slipped out of the back door. He felt confident he could talk more tomorrow. Well, maybe he could but only if he left now. Needing to decompress, he took Rukia for her walk while binging on Sword Art Online, a classic animated series that delighted and entertained him more every time he watched it.

As part of Anton's expectationality, he could only tolerate high-energy groups of people for a stint of time before his anxiety caused him to escalate emotionally inciting an inappropriate outburst or a shutdown. While walking the streets, he utilized a self-designed hybrid app on a pair of Smart glasses. This tool immersed him in an augmented reality simulation so he could fully enjoy the experience of gaming amalgamated with an app designed to guide the visually impaired by employing cameras, a gyroscope, GPS, OLED displays, and vibrating sensors to navigate for him. In this way, he could escape by watch a show or playing a video game while he traversed the city, oblivious to dangerous obstacles yet perfectly safe.

He ended up at Caribou Coffee, where he ordered a Nitro Turtle Mocha, a water cup, and a warm oatmeal cookie for his best girl. She took one sniff and turned her nose up at it, in no mood for a cookie when she could be napping in the condo. She was craving this perfect sliver of sunshine that hit the bed this time of the afternoon. Hours having passed, he noticed thunderheads forming and heard a bone-splitting thunder crack. Putting Rukia in her pup pack, he decided to jog home before the storm broke. Suddenly he realized she was missing her nap time. Anton worked in a cycle of short productive bursts that sometimes progressed into binges of working for 18 to 36-hour stints after which he would crashed for 24 hours or more. He went missing for a few days but he was usually holed up in his lair. Michaels had constant surveillance of him, which Anton wasn't wholly aware of. Still, seeing that he could no longer do any wrong, legally speaking, a modicum of digital supervision was a reasonable price.

CHAPTER SEVENTEEN

EXPERIENTIAL

AT 9:30 ON Thursday morning, he wandered tousle-haired back into the office into the newly assembled lab, followed dutifully by a drone carefully balancing cardboard drink carriers with piping hot coffee. Below that, on a modified appendage, hung a bag of muffins, bagels, and one quiche. To everyone's alarm, he had purchased and had delivered something similar to what they would have called in for themselves. Realizing that this kid not only had access to public records but probably knew the schedules by which they each evacuated their bowels. They shrugged and decided not to worry about something so minor, the gravity of what was occurring to the world coming to light.

"Let's breakfast in the conference room. Brief me." He commanded nonchalantly as he walked past them toward the back of the lab. He pushed on a tile of the east wall without explanation, promptly folded, and then opened on a hinge to take them into a smooth obsidian hallway. Dru, Anton's assistant, held open the door directly across from the easement and nodded. He winked at her as the drone hovered in front of her. Intelligently, it took the door's weight from her and plopped a small, triangular foot to lodge the door ajar. It then extended one metallic, skeletal arm and, with its digit, skillfully sliced an opening into the bag, revealing to Dru her pastry. She put her two hands on the side of the butler's canister-like head and gave him a kiss.

"Thank you, FROLO." She murmured. Alex, leading the party with one eyebrow cocked, turned around to see if the others were observing this momentous technology display. Evelyn crooned at the familiarity of Dru with the robot, and Adem simply muttered as he entered the room,

"Humboldts, let's start with you." Anton directed as he bit into some exotic pastry and sipped his Dark Mocha Java. The team listened intently while they grazed on the refreshments as the couple mentioned the scientific data that had corroborated Anton's theory.

"So, we suspect that that these animals have a territory based on the vicinity of the other megalodons." Evelyn explained

"When they are outside the range of any others, they are stimulated to metamorphize. It's nature's way of distributing them across a large surface area." Adem clarified.

"We haven't agreed that these are Otodus megalodon." She interjected

"What else could they be?" he brought up again.

"Well, a species which we never imagined, obviously." Justified TJ.

"-Or a megalodon is more a complex organism than we ever imagined. One in which the shark is only one of the forms of its life cycle. Whatever we choose to call them, these animals seem to defecate a type of ink, not unlike some modern-day species of jellyfish; however, their excrement is unique in that it contains the elements Cu and copper. Salt or NaClNaCl itself does not exist as a compound in water. The dissolution of salt in water means that the sodium cation and the chloride anion are separated and surrounded by water molecules. Therefore, no compound can bind to NaCl in water because NaClNaCl does not exist in water; however, possible that a compound "binds" with either sodium or chlorine. When this fecal compound dissipates in the saltwater, it forms a solid compound, copper chloride or CuClCuCl, denser and heavier than water. It clots forming a large membranous cloudy mass which quickly descends to the sea floor." Emmie added as she had been working closely with TJ on this theory. TJ chimed in.

"According to our simulations, this will likely have catastrophic environmental ramifications geologically, affecting the entire planet's ecosystem. When this stercus binds with salt and makes it fall to the ocean floor. From here, it will expeditiously alter the upper levels of the ocean H20, beginning in the Epipelagic Zone or Sunlight, the Mesopelagic Zone or Twilight, and finally, the Bthypelagic or Midnight Zone while the deepest levels. The Abyssoelagic and Hadal zones will be hypersaline, killing off all oceanic lifeforms.

"Saltwater is denser than freshwater. This change in pressure is predicted to cause the freshwater to flow into the rivers and lakes, triggering massive floods. With vegetation along the coasts drowning, this may generate an atmospheric cloud that could potentially incite mass extinction of all advanced species by reducing carbon dioxide. Furthermore, it's being predicted through environmental statistical analysis that this raises in freshwater levels from the oceans may ultimately generate rising temperatures and melt the polar icecaps. This phenomenon is likely to result in a die-off of the flora. As the root systems break down. Dust clouds, hills erode, and wind storms of dust cover block sunlight which causes the next ice age." Added Alex reluctantly.

"Also," Evelyn added, "This animal appears to be not only genetically related to modern immortal day jellyfish: Turritopsis dohrnii. The adult stage of this innovative creature grows, reaches adulthood, procreates: clones, and then, when it does not find enough nutrients, goes back into its amorphous stage.

"We could go as far as to hypothesize that if this species been trapped in that cavern for as long as we suspect, it could be the same age as crude oil. It could have been responsible for the Great Dying, a world-ending event pre-Homo sapien. We're talking 2.6 million years ago." Supplied Alex.

"Upon closer inspection, we have a running theory that the fossilized remains of the megalodon were just very small young adult specimens of this animal which through its life cycle ultimately lives infinitely." Remarked Emmie.

"Stage one of its Life cycle, nymph stages, it's amorphous blob floating around at the bottom of the ocean, or in this case, even below the crust, in a dormant stasis. Once it's disturbed, it enters stage two, when it floats to the top of the water's surface and forms a large blanket that feeds on plankton through osmosis and develops from stem cells in a two-celled thick plasma. Once nourished, it begins to develop due to ingestion of plankton and photosynthesis. It advances into a churning tube and then through different shapes. As it gains nourishment, develops into a jellyfish, and finally, morphs into its adult form, Stage Three is the shark, or what had previously called the megalodon." Explained Evelyn.

At this point, Anton took his heels off the conference table and sat upright. He pushed his glasses up onto his nose, took the last sip from his Caribou Java, grabbed the handles of his dog carrier bag, and got up.

"It's not a megalodon. It's an Infinydon." He concluded. With this realization, he pressed on a mirrored tile on the wall that popped open to reveal a mini-fridge where he had a small stash of string cheese and dried apricots. Peeling off a tiny tendril of cheese and dangling it into his mouth, he stated while chewing, "So, we are all going to die." He masticated while he ruminated. "Rukia," he called. His dog woke to attention and followed him as he exited the room through another hidden door that no one else was yet aware of. "Dru, tell Michaels that I'm implementing the Forbidden Fruit Fortification," he said on his way out. Raising his hand as a final salute to her and the team, he simply said, "Later, Nerds." and left the group.

The room burst into an uproar. Each team member proffered suggestions about what might be most important to do next. A helicopter left the landing pad to take Anton and Rukia to the master tree house he constructed and was waiting at the Klamath River Overlook in the Redwood Forest. His contract stated he and his companion would be transported to his safehouse once the researchers had been debriefed.

CHAPTER EIGHTEEN

ABANDON CAMP

DELSIN WAS PACKING up his campsite hurriedly, forced to abandon most of the accumulated belongings he had acquired over the summer. Upon arriving home this evening, he was greeted with a written warning from the sheriff's office, allowing him a brief time to vacate before the landowner returned with law enforcement and an order to arrest him for trespassing and littering. The slip read:

§11-22-123. Vagrancy: Universal Citation: 11 OK Stat § 11-22-123 (2014)

The municipal governing body may

provide by ordinance for the arrest, fine, and imprisonment of vagrants.

Dickwads. he thought as he packed his necessities into his rucksack. This bag was a lucky find early on his journey. It was lightweight yet roomy, breathable, and even water-resistant. There were days when it was his only shelter from the downpour. He made his way back to the road, feeling drawn toward the big city. There were undoubtedly more resources there. It was just so damn loud. After some mulling, he decided to stay in Oklahoma City until he felt driven out by a need for peace. Then, he would split again in search of another quiet place. To the city, it was.

Three days later, Delsin was set up at MacArthur Boulevard and Nineteenth Street in the Windsor Forrest neighborhood. He had gotten settled before dawn, put out his coffee can, and quickly fallen into a deep reverie. He began to rouse back to consciousness around 9:00 am in the morning to find a peculiar group of smiling faces sitting cross-legged in his vicinity. Two doors down, a woman who was perched delicately at a bistro set of the outdoor cafe, Cosmos Coffee, noticed him rousing and rushed toward him with a cold water bottle and a fresh scone wrapped in tissue paper of seraphim blue.

"He's back!" she had murmured to her companion as she left her post and came to his aid. He pulled away from her delicate hands when he noticed a blonde middle-aged woman threateningly close to him, touching his face. He flung his right arm out defensively, unaware of his surroundings knocking the crumbling pastry to the sidewalk. She yipped in alarm while tumbling back, trying to speak over his unease, telling him that she meant no harm. Resting back on his left forearm, he blinked, confused by his exultant audience.

"Delsin?" a silver-haired man crooned in a disarming tone approaching. "We're all wondering if you are okay." He explained as he crouched near the man but at a disarming distance. "My name is Gideon Richards, and I am with a small group, which is quickly growing," he gesticulated his arms wide," a group of men and women who wish to hear your divine message." Gideon paused as Del looked around the group and then back to the man. Delsin found his feet and took a few steps back. "Delsin, Don't be alarmed. The group and I would like to help you. We watched videos of your ... speeches online, and we want to know more of your divine knowledge." Failing to process precisely what videos this man might be referring to, Delsin looked from one alien face to the next, all beaming joyfully. He didn't understand what they could be smiling about since his message was not one of joy. It was one of macabre abuse toward our earth and how she, Mother Earth, was coming to exterminate us to take our power away. She planned to recycle mankind, the most destructive species on the planet, so she and all of her other inhabitants may live. Unable to conceive the intentions of this group and disquieted by their blissful semblance, he ran. He ran away from all of them. He fled, hidden. He hoped they'd never find him.

Delsin walked all day erratically without pausing to find sustenance and, well after sundown, ran out of gas near the doors of a nondescript shelter that he felt might be just as covert as any place. He entered and was offered a shower and a cot but no food. Freshly bathed, his empty stomach turned in knots with famine. He ignored that familiar sensation, pulling his clean but tangled hair off his forehead as he reclined onto the too-short cot, attempting to quiet his mind for the night when Gideon walked into the dimly lit room. The man had resources and had been surveilling him. He had been notified the moment Delsin was admitted.

This time, he approached the young man more prudently. Delsin immediately sat up and stood rigidly at attention, the muscles in his neck visibly pulsating as his blood pressure began to rise. Gideon held his hands palm out in front of himself to indicate pacification while he pulled up a chair and dragged it near the cot but with a respectable amount of space. He stated that he wished for Delsin to sit in the chair next to him, which he did not.

"It's okay." he began amicably. "I'm not here to offer you anything that you don't willfully choose to accept, Son. I want nothing from you but to better understand your message." He paused, but Delsin did not say anything in return. He went on. "Videos of you have been popping up. One video went viral. Then other people began recording you and posting to an account that a woman began in your honor after you spoke of catastrophic events that had yet to be on the news, which came to light afterward. This helped us understand that the information you give is truly inspired. Your mother and sister saw them and have been corresponding with the group, hoping to establish contact with you. The coalition is based out of New York. We have an apartment for you there where you can meditate in peace, and we can meet all of your physical needs so you can focus on divination in the hopes that we can understand and make amends with your Mother Earth." He paused, giving the man a few minutes to digest this information. Delsin began to relax in consideration and tensed visibly in suspicion. "Listen, Son, a Greenbucks account was opened for you so the public could donate to the cause of your care so you could focus on your ability in the safety of a home without fear of judgment or danger. It already has only 1.2 million dollars in it that legally belongs to you. The woman who tried to feed you breakfast is the trustee, but she can only pay your taxes, not withdraw any funds." He paused, attempting to read the stoic young man but getting nothing. "Let me at least buy you dinner so we can talk. I know you haven't eaten today." At that suggestion, his stomach let out a loud rumble, and Delsin felt like listening to this guy was at least worth a meal. He would eat as much as possible, and Delsin figured he could kick his ass if he got pervy. This guy was old, he considered, like 60. He grabbed his pack and stood up, sliding his feet into his unlaced boots, and shrugged in acceptance toward the offer of a hot meal. Gideon sat waiting for verbal acknowledgment, so there was no room for misunderstanding.

"Well, old man, let's go."

CHAPTER NINETEEN

DIRTY MAGAZINE

THE AFTERNOON COURTYARD was sun-dappled by the shade trees of the Holy Trinity Parish. Playful sunbeams danced in the serene water of the large fountain. The harmony of birdsong and the rushes of the wind on the treetops dulled the bustling noise pollutants of the city, dulling it into innocuous white noise. For that reason and many more, Father Johnson loved it here. He sat on the fountain, finally spilling his guts about what he'd been experiencing while Father Bromley pruned the rose bushes, seeming not to listen as he clipped the hedges. Knowing that his comrade was almost entirely deaf, he felt comfortable speaking his mind with no fear of judgment. No matter what was said, Father Bromley would nod and smile in concession.

"This thing is massive. It seems to grow bigger every day. I can tell because she can eat anything, and then this is the weirdest part. She seems cognizant of her digestion. When she defecates, it's like she's passing an eighteen-wheeler. It's so dense and heavy, but come to think of it, really only after exposure to the water. The salt in the water is turbulently absorbed by the stool for a few minutes. When it reaches a certain saturation point, the whole mess sinks like a boulder, and I can feel the water in my own lungs changing, becoming less alkaline, but it doesn't alarm her; she's built for it. All those other sea creatures aren't. They're flailing around, dying. They look like they're like little astronauts that lost their helmets. They're dying, and she's just watching them flail around. She cares for their loss, which makes her sad, but she knows it's all for the greater good, but you know who she's really after, man! Do you know how people say that Great Whites are man-eaters? They're not. Sometimes a person just gets in their way. This lady is looking for humans to kill. She is being driven on a mission to kill people. It's pretty frightening, but we're safe as long as we stay out of the water. It makes me nervous that we live on the coast, but I wouldn't go swimming any time soon.

A loud rap from an upstairs window got their attention. "Father Johnson!" the

Monsignor called in admonition from his office window. "Don't you have an appointment to attend?" He hollered from the third-story window, pointing to his watch. His disapproval of his parishioner flagrantly sharing his supernatural experience with his peers was apparent. He was experiencing some regret over giving Johnson so much time off as now he was busying himself through idle chitchat and exploring supernatural theories over what may be happening to him.

"Yes, Monsignor. I was just preparing to leave." He defended, waving one hand over his head. He began making dramatic movements toward gathering himself to leave until he saw the shadow leave the windowsill; he settled himself back on the fountain.

"So, do you think this monster is God?"

Father Bromley asked him outright.

"I couldn't say. It feels distinctly female. Could the Almighty be a woman after all?" The two men tittered at such a ludicrous notion. Animated by his conscience for partaking in this harmless yet exciting guilty pleasure of confabulation, Chris looked at the window and saw the Monsignor glaring down at him with his arms crossed over a protruding belly, especially pronounced from the downward vantage. Masking snickers at being caught challenging his superior, he nervously hopped up in a manner more reticent of a mischievous pupil than a middle-aged man. Mirthful at being caught and pointing to his peer to avert blame. Father Bromley turned to see their admonisher at the window glaring sternly; Chris genuinely made motions to head out while his cohort pointed back at Chris shaking his head in disagreement, unwilling to share the condemnation.

Hours later, Chris sat naked, except for an examining gown, cheeks perched uncomfortably on a hospital clinic cot, awaiting his results. He picked at his nails and surveyed the room for the hundredth time. In the last ninety minutes, he had his blood drawn for a complete blood panel, injected a tracer agent, instructed to void his bladder and urinated into a plastic cup, and laid to rest in a coffin-like PET-CT bed. It was nerve-wracking to listen to a series of buzzing and clicking sounds and lie unmoving for over an hour. Plagued by unnerving thoughts.

"It's definitely a tumor. I read about it on Web MD, which would explain the headaches and his loss of sanity.' he grumbled aloud. When no one argued counter-wise, he resigned to lay back and try to relax. As he was dosing off, an annoyingly pretty nurse came in just long enough to compel him to sit up. She smiled and set down a Dixie cup of tap water so that he could rehydrate. He retrieved the cup and sat back down. Swallowing the metallic-tasting liquid, he scrunched his nose, crumpled the cup, and tossed it toward the wastebasket. He missed. Staring at the cup lying on the floor, it seemed to mock him. He peered closer, taking notice of some hair and fuzz just behind the counter's overhang. Nasty, he thought, shivering a little. I've never been an athlete, he acknowledged sadly. Contemplating how many baskets he'd made in his life? None? Had he really made zero baskets in his whole life?

"That seems a shame," he maundered. "Maybe I should make just one before this cancer puts me in my grave." He announced to the duty mannequin, modeling the circulatory system in the corner. He scooted off the table, his bare feet slapping on the cold tiled floors. He clumsily reached down over his paunch and teetered before grabbing the cup. He took five steps back to the door and held both hands up, poised to shoot. Tongue sticking out in concentration, he flicked his wrist and made the shot with a tiny hop. It fell eighteen inches shy of the basket. He glowered at the cup as if asking why it was so ungainly. Shrugging, he shuffled forward and, with his foot, scooted the rubbish tucking it out of sight, knocking his big toe into the counter, wincing. Growling some forbidden four-letter words, he climbed back atop the examining table.

Having already studied the charts of the human nasal system on the wall extensively, he resorted to thumbing through a Cosmo magazine that promised to teach him ten tips for having a Hot Girl Summer! What does that mean, he mused? Disappointed that this was the only entertainment offered to one waiting for the physician's return, he opened to the first glossy page to see a pale-skinned girl with an unnatural pout in a back-breaking pose. She wore stilettos, a long skirt, and a... bra? Was this young lady in underwear? he questioned. He could actually see her... nipples! No! Surely not. He reasoned. Holding the image closer, he squinted more thoroughly with sweaty palms to examine the photograph.

They were peachy, he observed. His eyebrows raised in disbelief.

"I can't look at this!" He proclaimed aloud, slapping the magazine closed and attempting to think of holy things. He thought of the regal leaders of the church, then the Gospels, and passages that spoke of Esther and Mary Magdalene. Were their breasts like budding rosebuds too? His mind raced, thoughts escalating. His hospital gown began to display a small but proud tent. He pulled anxiously at the garment and visualized how hot hell might be after this tumor ended his life. But then again, there were immoral women there. Ugh! YES! Demon temptresses. Not attractive! STOP! He told himself while waiting for the doctor to return to read his results.

Suddenly, a sharp knock on the door interrupted his sadist introspection. He sat soberly, listening to the Indian doctor trying to decipher his meaning through his accent. His eyes refocused on the waxy litter of the Dixie cup as the doctor explained all the typical results of his blood tests and PET scan.

"We did not notice any bright spots that would reveal higher levels of chemical activity to give us a clue about how your tissues and organs function. A specialist will read your exam and mail you the detailed report, but I told Monsignor Bell that I would offer you my preliminary opinion today. You are fine except for stress related sleep disorder. Here is a prescription for Somnafil. This will sedate you so you can get some rest. I've already called the Monsignor and told him that you need your sabbatical extended by two weeks so you can get some rest and get well again. Do you have any questions?" the doctor asked.

"I guess not." The baffled man uttered. Shifting his weight in preparation to dismount the table to pick up that contemptuous cup and then get dressed.

CHAPTER TWENTY

STRATEGEM

THE TEAM WAS settling in the conference room around a meal of deli sandwiches in another late-night think tank session before they broke for a respite to get some shut-eye.

"You start." Dru pointed at Evelyn to kick off the meeting.

"Oh!" Evelyn covered her mouth, relishing a delicious mouthful. Holding a finger up, she pantomimed the chewing motion asking for a moment.

"Well, I love deli," she said with a mouthful. "Okay. So, other than mass destruction and all that mayhem," she opened, dabbing the dressing from the corner of her mouth, "we see significant changes globally. Regions worldwide are experiencing increased temperatures causing glacial retreat, decreasing snow cover, and shrinking ice sheets. Consequently, the oceans are getting warmer and more acidic and rising to the point of flooding. Marine life dying off by the gazillions.

"So, we can soon expect this activity to precip more severe weather events: hurricanes, tsunamis, torrential rains, hail, snow, and flooding, tornadoes, dust storms, earthquakes, and in extreme circumstances, volcanic eruptions." Dru contributed. Alex took a slug of his drink and set it down, bringing their attention back to more immediate issues.

"I think we need to focus on what's happening now rather than theorizing on what may happen in the future. Other than a monster killing people, the changes to the ocean is the most pressing issue. This alteration is killing all the wildlife. Once the fauna has been wiped out, what will happen next? When the whole chemical composition of the ocean has been changed, what will become of our planet? And what is this *thing* under the water, terrorizing and devouring everything in its path? Whatever it is, it's primal, ancient, driven by instinct." Dru entered with FROLO in toe.

"Well, we can safely assume that temperatures will continue to rise due to the greenhouse effect." Emmie elaborated, thinking aloud.

"Global Warming? That's the danger for us on land? Isn't that supposed to occur over hundreds or thousands of years, after I'm dead?" Alex asked with a mouthful. Dru countered.

"Well, we have been basing those estimates on our current ecosystem and environmental circumstances. Our biosphere has just changed. A new, influential predator is changing things faster than any other species in recorded history," Dru contributed. Having conveyed her thought, she dipped her sandwich deep into the bath of steaming au jus and took a heaping bite with broth dripping carelessly as if their species were not in mortal danger. FROLO rolled forward, dabbing at her chin with a napkin with one skeletal arm.

"The idea that this species might have

been responsible for the last mass extinction is disturbing," TJ interjected.

"Also, we decided this thing is a Carcharocles megalodon?" Adem asked of the group based on fossilized records cross referenced with DNA.

"An Infinydon." Evelyn redressed.

"Where did that come from?" TJ asked.

"That's what I named it. It's a real lusus naturae," Anton announced cryptically.

"Fossils of this animal in the young stage were deemed the Carcharocles megalodon but this thing is not what we believed the meg to be. The largest fossils we have found were 60 feet long which is three times the size of a great white." Adem answered.

"This animal that we are pursuing now has already exceeded the size of a Balaenoptera musculus, the modern-day blue whale, which has been documented at over 100 feet long or 30 meters long. This thing may be twice that size." Evelyn added.

"Megalodon was believed to have gone extinct, I don't know, 20 million years ago in the Pliocene Epoch. This thing has an *infinite* life cycle." Dru pointed out.

"If that's the case, how do we have fossilized remains of the them if they can't die?" Alex contested pointing out a blaring flaw in the argument."

"We talked about that yesterday. The only theory we have at this point is that they are vulnerable in their young adult form and can be killed if they are threatened during that window of time but at the size she's at now, I fear that window has closed." Emmie explained.

"Do we all agree?" Emmie asked of the group. "On the name Carcharocles infinydon?"

"Aye!" Each nodded, holding up their right hand, mumbling in agreement while chewing.

"Most importantly, how do we stop it?" Emmie asked, which caused the room to be quiet as each member thought operatively without any solid ideas.

"Guys! We need a plan!" Anton pressed.

CHAPTER TWENTY ONE

PENTHOUSE

DELSIN CLOSED HIS laptop from the sofa in his penthouse in the Convivium Complex on 86th Street in New York City. He had just finished another interview by webcam where he was being asked about the sudden glacial retreat and the shrinking ice sheets. Del wasn't there in person because he was refusing to travel anymore. He said every second of his time was precious, and he was left debilitated on many days, with his visions coming more frequently and fervently these weeks. He dialed his phone.

"Del. You were great! I think we

were able to express our message clearly. People are getting it. They are changing! How do you feel?" Gideon asked supportively.

"No more interviews," Delsin said. "It's too late for change. I'll keep streaming my visions for the followers but no more interviews." He paused to hear silence on the other end, Gideon playing his hand by not speaking. "People don't believe me, and besides, we're out of time." Delsin said depressively. His eyes wandered out the windows at the rising water level of the ocean and then at the bedroom doors behind which his mother and sister were peacefully resting. "All the beaches are underwater even at a low tide, and we've had more tidal waves coming in now that we're getting nearer to the full moon. Man has lived. We …. abused our power. Our time has come to an end. I'm ready." The other end of the line remained quiet.

"Well, that's dark." Gideon finally returned. "So, what can we do?" he asked, concern in his voice.

"We can give thanks for our time, express gratitude. We can meditate on our next destination, but we can no longer stay here," the young man explained. Gideon held his breath on the other end of the line. "That's what I've been telling you, people." Again, Gideon was at a loss for words.

"What encouragement can you offer a man in touch with the universe who's just been given the memo that our extinction was booked and scheduled?" He asked. Delsin failed to respond. "How much time?" he asked, thoughtfully digesting the gravity of this new reality.

"Weeks. Days, maybe." Delsin guessed. "I don't know, Man."

"Well, your rent is paid up until the end of this year. The place is all yours. Do you need anything else from me?" Gideon asked as a last service of duty. "I'm going to spend time with my daughters and grandkids. And soon enough maybe I'll be with my late wife again." His voice grew thick with emotion. Taking a deep breath, he said thoughtfully, "Well, I guess we all will." he inserted, defeated, attempting to sound half as brave as the young warrior. "Well, call if you want to, but I'll not schedule anything more. I'm going to stop working and just spend time living." He explained. "You know, I've always wanted to touch a snake, like a giant python?" Delsin raised one eyebrow at this confession. "And try French wine and soak in a hot tub naked. I think I'll do those things too." Gideon confessed. Delsin smiled at this.

"You do that." With that, the conversation was over. Delsin looked at the coalition secretary's notification on his laptop that a priest wanted to meet with him.

"No more appointments." Delsin wrote back and changed his email setting to Do Not Disturb. He turned on the television and immediately muted it to silence the shrieking coming from the news showing a montage of exotic resorts deep underwater. There were other stories of freak storms, volcanic eruptions, and earthquakes. Then came footage of the recovered wreckage of that cruise liner and meteorologists excitedly predicting crisis while discouraging panic. Shaking his head in sorrow, he clicked off the power and stood at the window, watching the waves pound at the buildings previously a few blocks from the beach. He thought about how difficult his time on this earth had been but thanked the Great Spirits for his gift. He apologized for his past actions while trying to quiet their voices. He was glad to be free of alcohol now. Since being put up in a safe place where he could rest, get regular sustenance, and allow his visions to occur whenever necessary, he no longer had such disabling headaches. He watched the surf pound the abandoned beachfront properties from his windows. After a few minutes, he detected the sensation that another episode was coming on.

He logged onto the YouTube channel the group had designated and set his computer to live stream. He took a long swig of water and sat on the floor in front of his couch for support to ensure that he wouldn't fall. He did his best to relax, propping two pillows behind his head, leaning his head back, and allowing nature to take its course.

Within sixty seconds, 32,804 viewers were online, hundreds of which were typing furiously in the chat to him and each other.

"Marry me, Buck!" -hawtToddy22

"Were gonna dye." -Freddy$unds

"Hi, Sara! U there?" -FaithHope&Love

"I wuz 1st" -CandieKane

"It's 2 funcking hot out here! Wtf?" DrHungover

"What u going to say 2day, Delsun?" -Shaggydawg

"I'm going to go surfing today, dare me" Drummerdude

"Git me pregs, segsy." SunnyDeed

"This is happening because of the polar icecaps are melting" Flowrgurl.

"No itsbecuz of evil people going to hail." -JohnieBeegood

The nonsensical chat feed went on and on, moving so fast that no one could read it. There were people dropping money and proclamations of love and hate for Delsin. Some were making predictions about today's session, but few listened as his head rose and he began to recite the ancient wisdom on the Great Spirits. Hearing his moans and cries crescendo, his mother emerged from her room and saw that he was safe, just in cogitation. Taking care not to walk into the camera frame, she sat across from him on the other couch, tucking her long ebony hair behind her ear, watching her son, the miracle, the seer, the one who knows things. Clutching the talisman around her neck, she said her own kind of prayer in thanks for the sacred vessel born of her womb. She sat back, legs folded beneath her, watching her baby boy contort with distress as divine messages were passed from his body and out of his mouth. She wept, listening to the message he delivered.

CHAPTER TWENTY TWO

STEAK TARTARE

DRU ENTERED THE lab mid-morning with FROLO in tow delivering coffee. Having worked until three the previous morning, they had all agreed not to report today until nine because rest was paramount in pursuing such revolutionary intellectual exploration. Evelyn, Emmie, and TJ worked with Anton at his central processing unit, running stratagem simulations. Alex was off examining water samples under the microscope.

"Yes!" TJ trumpeted at the most recent replication.

"Thank you," Emmie said graciously, turning at the scent of steaming joe, smirking with self-satisfaction. Evelyn simply reached out behind her without taking her eyes off the screen.

"This could work!" she announced. "This could actually work!"

"What could work?" asked Adem, just reporting for duty, scrubbing his hands over his face and rubbing sleep away.

"Well, good morning, Sleeping Beauty!" she greeted him, jumping up excitedly and tiptoeing to plop a quick kiss on his scratchy chin. He sweetly patted the top of her head to acknowledge her affection while still letting her know he needed a few more minutes to reciprocate. With a polite nod, he snatched his chai from out of the drink carrier, potent ginger and cinnamon wafting, and mounted the nearest stool. He took a cautious sip, gauging the heat. Unscathed, he took a deeper pull while admiring his wife across the lab, appreciating how extraordinary she was even when a little disheveled from sleep deprivation: lopsided bun and makeup-bare skin, casual jeans, and tennis shoes. Leaning toward her, he left a quick kiss on her temple before moving over to her side and, in a sleep-rasped voice, asked,

"Well, what did I miss?"

"Just watch!" she nudged her shoulder into his chest. At the sound of this excitement and suddenly compelled by the motivation of caffeine, Alex got up from his microscope. Cup in one hand, high-fiving Dru with his free hand and fist-bumping FROLO, he strode over to see what was happening on the monitor. They all watched in suspense as the animation progressed with the beacon signal luring the shark. Just as the beast consumed the target, BOOM! She was injected with a cryogenic solution that would turn her into ice.

"So, according to your Doppler readings of her biorhythms, this will really draw her into the snare," Dru asked the lady doctor, "As long as we can properly emit this frequency?"

"We'll need some serious darts to inject that massive bitch!" FROLO chimed in with a robotic voice, not unlike Bumblebee's. Everyone in the team turned and looked at the cybernetic organism.

"You can talk?" Adem asked incredulously. They all broke into hysterical gaiety; their joy was prompted by this remarkable finding but hearing the robot say something so casual had them all enlivened with celebration!

"You know, we've been living in this lab for seventeen days, and there are so many amazing restaurants in DC. Let's go to lunch and celebrate while there is still civilized life on Earth. Well, come right back afterward and work on a plan for implementation, after a long lunch," suggested Alex.

"Yeah. It will be like a Last Supper," Dru lamented morosely.

"Dark," said TJ.

"Here, here," the team said, raising their disposable cups all but Evelyn.

"But, should we really quit now?" she queried aloud.

"We're not quitting, just taking a short break: two hours," Adem clarified in a coddling tone. "I'll set a timer," he promised.

She tried batting him away as he put arms around her to guide her outside the lab. She continued weakly resisting, naturally tempted by the idea of tantalizing cuisine. He turned to face her, putting his rough hands on her cheeks.

"Sweet Pea, everything will be fine," he assured her. He hugged her tight and kissed her pursed lips cutting off any further argument. Wrapped in his arms, she went limp. She began to giggle and then went quiet. Arms wrapped around his neck, she asked, quavering into his ear.

"Make love to me tonight?"

"You can bet your life on it," he answered back. She smiled tenderly and then grimaced, considering the figure of speech in which one bets on another's life, dire times as these were. He cunningly set his timer for three hours while FROLO ordered a car, saying he was going to slam a tequila shot.

"You drink," TJ asked the droid, now in even greater disbelief?

"I'll take that shaken, not stirred," FROLO responded in the distinguished voice of James Bond. The Brain Trust all erupted into laughter as they headed off for a bit of much-needed downtime. So, they could travel as a group, FROLO ordered a limo where the festivities began. The group agreed upon Brasserie Liberté. While being chaffered, they sipped champagne and stretched out, letting go of their cares. Upon arrival, the group was ushered into a private room with a plethora of attendants.

They began jubilantly by sharing hors

d'oeuvres from each other's plates as a family would. They sipped French onion soup gratinée, nibbled petite salad with green peppercorn sauce, on steak tartare, ornate quail eggs, escargots sauvages de Bourgogne, and warm baguettes while sipping complimentary spirits. Agreeing to discuss anything but work, they unwound as the wait staff continued to bring out tantalizing treasure. They sampled sumptuous dishes drowned liberally in savory sauces and partook of ambrosial wines as the hours passed. As the afternoon ebbed, they imbibed flavorful sparkling drinks with mouthwatering smoked gruyère, mornay with brandade croquettes, macaroni au gratin, and burrata with toasted hazelnuts, pomegranate seeds, orange segments, and light basil oil.

As they became somewhat inebriated, they recounted their interpretations of each other in those first few days chortling at FROLO's remarkable impersonations that pegged them each impeccably. They were amused by his uncanny ability to replay key moments of their interactions intuitively to capture their individuality. It was bizarre to observe this automaton performing their parodies in each humorous manner.

It made Evelyn retrospectively consider the implication of the machine's surviving this event while humans became extinct, potentially becoming the next overseer of our world. Shaking her head, she dismissed the idea with the concluding hope that, in that case, they were more considerate of harmony with nature instead of exploitation and dominance. The afternoon passed, and as Dru picked off the last crumbs of Alex's cheesecake from his plate, Adem pushed back his chair and proposed a toast. Evelyn held up her glass and tapped, making three brilliant chimes. The party all fell to attention all eyes on the tall, strapping scientist.

"A month ago, I never would have dreamed to be dining in such a fine place with such an assembly of such gentility coming up with a master plan to save the world. No matter what may come, I will cherish this time that we have had together and for the love that I share with my wife." Everyone began to nod in agreement. "To the Turds!" Adem proclaimed.

"To the turds!" everyone repeated in jubilation, laughing, clinking glasses, hugging, and making half-drunken merry. Suddenly, Michaels pushed through the door with the squat yet fastidious restaurant manager trailing after him exhibiting an argument contrary to his actions that he had presidential orders that this party was not to be disturbed. Noting his dampened brow and sour expression, the party grew quiet. FROLO stood and, with one metallic skeletal hand at his temple, stood rigidly as if in respectful salute.

"FROLO," greeted the commander with a nod but no return salute. "We have-"

"Good morning, Vietnam! This is not a test. This is rock and roll. Time to rock it from the delta to the DMZ!" FROLO belted out over a loudspeaker in Robin William's voice, mocking Michael's militaristic disposition.

The entire room lost it, sending the team and serving staff into uproarious laughter that had them all howling until their faces were tear-streaked. Even Michaels had to smile at his mischievous impersonation.

"If you've all finished your brunch…" tapping his crystal faced-watch. The group began shuffling around, wiping their faces on soft linen and pushing their plates away, mildly to moderately inebriated. They simultaneously reached behind them and under the tables for their bags as the wait staff hastily delivered overcoats and sweaters. As they left their cozy alcove, they could see through the glass front visage of the dining room that the weather had taken a nasty turn, and another menacing storm was blowing in, causing the trees to bend and bow in the horizontal rain. A darkness fell over the group that sobered them up while on the somber ride back to the lab.

CHAPTER TWENTY THREE

EXODUS

FATHER JOHNSON WAS certainly skeptical of the doctor's report of his health and wellness. Despite the narrative he'd been raised to believe, he had begun to question the notion that he may have a direct connection with God. Were these visions the insight he was subconsciously looking for? No. Surely not. Was this the devil, he pondered? Maybe, it's the work of demons that have been invited because of my lack of faith, he contemplated, sickened. He sat, clad in his sweat-soaked bathrobe, no longer enjoying his downtime. Devoid of his daily routine, his days were now plagued with fitful bouts of sleep with no productivity, and his nights were anything but restful. He was having intense visions every day.

What he was experiencing became more surreal each time he witnessed first-hand the destruction of the known world. He had observed each phase of this creature's life as she developed. Even in her primitive form, he vividly perceived a consciousness. Although ancient, this was not her first life cycle on our planet. She had killed off civilizations before, advanced societies of other top predators who had simply lived their course. He smacked his tongue, which felt as dry as cotton and drank from the glass of water from his nightstand before noticing the tiny moth drowned in it. He gasped; now sure he could taste the dust of the wing scale in his mouth. Grouching, he toasted a bagel and propped up his phone to check his YouTube notifications. He had recently acquired several subscriptions to a sundry of channels that covered the catastrophe in one way or another.

The first time he saw an event reported that he had telepathically witnessed himself, he became dizzy at the implications, confirming his looming misgiving that all of this was real. It was then that he flushed those sleeping pills. He suspected they weren't stopping the night terrors, just erasing his memory of them upon waking. Maybe, his experience was significant, somehow, he reasoned.

Mind awhirl, with one ear cocked toward the video describing the escalating predictions, he snatched his bagel from the toaster. Tossing it from one toasty finger to the other, crumbs fell underneath dry-skinned shuffling feet with slightly yellow toenails. Having traveled the four steps from the countertop to the table-for-one, he plopped his paltry meal onto the table, crumbs splaying in all directions. Tongue sticking out in concentration, he topped his pastry with an excess of blueberry cream cheese while gazing fixedly at his phone. With one chubby finger, he clicked on the notification that Fiero's World News had published in their Friday episode. He clicked on it and began listening to a blurb about a man named Delsin Buck. This man, Chris distinguished, seemed to be suffering a similar affliction. Against his churning gut, he jotted down the email address into the margin of his leather-bound Bible in the book of Jeremiah near where God says that he has plans for us to prosper and not to harm us and for us not to give up hope for a future. Until we mess up? Christopher wondered, considering the last Exodus: the flood. Pushing through hesitation, he hastily composed a message to this young man telling him everything he knew and begged for a meeting with him. His hope was to confirm, even from a lunatic, that he wasn't crazy.

CHAPTER TWENTY FOUR

MODEST MEASURE

ALEX ENJOYED THE sweet aroma of his steaming pecan roast, which Dru had picked up but rolled his eyes at the bedroom eyes that Evelyn was giving Adem from across the lab.

"Get a room, you two!" he finally said. TJ looked up from his simulation, smiling and making subtle eye contact with Emmie.

"I think it's sweet!" Emmie said, smirking shyly.

"We all need to be finding joy wherever we can right now because we know not what might happen next." Dru proffered wisely, youthful eyebrows raised at her elders.

"Not a month, Guys. Try about seventeen days." TJ said.

"Seventeen days until what?" Alex queried.

"According to my system's analysis, based on the oceanic soil and water samples we've received, my data indicates that we have less than three weeks before irreparable changes have been made to our planet." He said, looking up and at each of them. "Mass extinction event, not just of people, but all advanced lifeforms." Explained TJ.

"Um…Everybody, you should come and see this!" Dru called from the extensive workstation at the far end of the room. We just received this footage. Apparently, Anton has still been working from his safehouse in the trees. Check out this broadcast from the

Voyage Data Recorder from the Bonnie Baroness."

"Who?" Alex asked

"That ship that went missing." Adem reminded him. The grAlex enjoyed the sweet aroma of his steaming pecan roast, which Dru had picked up but rolled his eyes at the bedroom eyes that Evelyn was giving Adem from across the lab.

"Get a room, you two!" he finally said. TJ looked up from his simulation, smiling and making subtle eye contact with Emmie.

"I think it's sweet!" Emmie said, smirking shyly.

"We all need to be finding joy wherever we can right now because we know not what might happen next." Dru proffered wisely, youthful eyebrows raised at her elders.

"Not a month, Guys. Try about seventeen days." TJ said.

"Seventeen days until what?" Alex queried.

"According to my system's analysis, based on the oceanic soil and water samples we've received, my data indicates that we have less than three weeks before irreparable changes have been made to our planet." He said, looking up and at each of them. "Mass extinction event, not just of people, but all advanced lifeforms." Explained TJ.

"Um…Everybody, you should come and see this!" Dru called from the extensive workstation at the far end of the room. We just received this footage. Apparently, Anton has still been working from his safehouse in the trees. Check out this broadcast from the

Voyage Data Recorder from the Bonnie Baroness."

"Who?" Alex asked

"That ship that went missing." Adem reminded him. The group assembled, sitting on stools. TJ and Emmie perched on the countertop, and he stood near enough to pick up the scent of her coconut shampoo. For just a moment, he studied her features as she watched the screen, long lashes casting a shadow down her cheek. Her cheeks flushed slightly, and she demurely tucked her loose hair behind her ear. Knowing he was caught, he broke his gaze.

"Wait! Stop it right there. Look at how long her fins are. She has the longer fins a body than a modern-day blue shark." Evelyn said.

"Yeah. It's huge!" agreed Alex.

"Yes, but look," said Adem approaching the monitor. "Her fins are massive compared to a Great White of comparable size. She's actually shaped a little more like a blue shark."

"What happened to her face?" asked TJ.

"There's that too," noted Dru. Her snout or rostrum is incredibly short but measuring this, she has a jaw span of about 30 feet, and in this still, I can count over 250 teeth which are about twelve to twenty inches in length."

"That's fucking terrifying," responded Alex very unscientifically. "And it seems like she had an especially gross attitude too. Can you tell the gender?" he asked inquisitively.

"I'm not seeing a pair of claspers, a male identifier in many modern sharks." Examined Evelyn. "More importantly, can she buccal pump? If so, she won't need to be submerged to breath."

"I'm guessing so." Adem observed, "because she's already been out of the water for five minutes and doesn't seem compromised."

"She seems to be calculating." Emmie pointed out in alarm, taking a closer look.

"I'm looking at her dermal denticles." Evelyn was puzzled, honing in on the subtle color shift.

"A shark's skin, or shagreen, is like a cat's tongue. Rough from one direction but slick from the other, which helps them slide through the water.

"Would that be hydrodynamics?" Alex asked.

"Precisely," Evelyn responded absently, still questioning whether or not those scales were changing tone.

As the film played out, demonstrating the catastrophe, the team members took turns covering their mouths and muttered obscenities. When the beast came into view, Dru paused the image, and simulated measurements were taken.

"The Infinydon is estimated to be three hundred, fifty-six feet long."

"That can't be right!" TJ said.

"That measurement is a modest estimate overcompensating for perspective," Dru responded. The rest of the footage was watched in silence, with the group huddled together in solidarity. Evylyn was paralyzed facing the gravity of what they were up against, never becoming more apparent.

Adem was the first to speak once it was

over. "I need a blue print of her anatomy, the best we can concoct so we can engineer a ambush."

"We have to trap her." Evelyn agreed. "I was hoping if we just raised her out of the water, nature would take its course, but she doesn't seem phased by being immersed. I wouldn't imagine she could tolerate being beached for an extended period because of her weight. Controlling her is going to be challenging.

"She has to die," Alex said, taking the last swig of his coffee and tossing the cup in the garbage in a defiant act of finality.

Dru returned from the bathroom with her kinky curls into a fresh pony tale and said, "Take a short recess. Conference Room in Ten. Team, we're going to have to kill this primordial bitch!"

After spending a few minutes regrouping, the group trickled in and saw a list of facts on the monitor that they already knew about her.

Adem began, "I would just like to say for the record, as a scientist, it only seems ethical to collect her and study her at least for a while,"

"But," Evelyn broke it, "We've realized beyond a reasonable doubt that she's far too dangerous, and we don't have the resources to house or care for an animal as powerful and massive as she."

"So, we agree that we have to kill her?" TJ asked.

"Well, it will be her or us," Emmie said.

"Just for a moment," Alex broke in,

"Let's try to think of this objectively. Is it possible that we have lived out our reign as the dominant lifeform on this planet?"

"I'll agree that we've been pretty terrible stewards of this place the last few hundred years." Evelyn resolved.

"As far as we can tell, scientifically, we've been the worst keepers this planet has ever had. We're the only species in known history to indiscriminately waste, kill each other with little to no discretion, damage our environment to the evocation of climate change, and to cause the extinction of innumerable species of flora and fauna." -TJ agreed.

"So, what are you guys saying? That maybe our time as a lifeform is over?" Emmie asked incredulously.

"I'm just saying that we have a responsibility to consider the ramifications of our situation and our actions scientifically, intelligently. We should try to remove each of ourselves from the equation and consider solutions mathematically." Adem clarified.

"If we win this war, what are the chances mankind will survive the foreseeable future in light of our destructive habits?" Evelyn examined.

"It has already been calculated and established that our earth's destruction is imminent. There is another team who's researching colonization of other planets. We are already preparing for our planet's demise as a direct result of human behavior." Dru remarked.

"So… if we win this war and live, it may

only be for a brief time. Not only will we kill ourselves, but likely most other lifeforms on this planet as well." Alex acquiesced.

"Is it not too late to change?" Adem debated really not liking the turn of this conversation.

"Our behavioral change would have to be radical." Emmie rationalized. "We have overpopulated the planet. We would have to alter our way of life almost completely and go back to living off the land in harmony with nature and learn to stop taking beyond what the earth willingly gives us. Also, we would have to do away with burning fossil fuels and only use renewable energies. We would have to stop mass agriculture and using chemicals and pesticides. Of course, we would have to stop polluting and creating undue waste."

"I hate to say this, but people would never agree to do that if they have a choice." Due said. "Many people would rather stick their heads in the sand and ignorantly believe that if this situation is not going to affect them directly today, they are not willing to give up comfort to make the change."

"Tony Robbins said it best when he said that Change happens when the pain of staying the same is greater than the pain of change." Adem affirmed. "The pain of what will happen eventually is too great for most people to even fathom."

"Yes, but, on the other hand, we must also consider that it does seem to go against our biology as the dominant life form to just lay down before our competitor even if that seems like the ethical choice? Isn't that urge to fight and kill not an integral part of our innate biology encouraging us to prevail? Isn't that a shining example of the theory of survival of the fittest? If we survive this, maybe it proves that we are intelligent lifeforms that can make progress!" Alex suggested.

"I guess," Emmie articulated, "that would be demonstrated by which species wins and where they go from there."

"May the best species win." Evelyn declared in a somber tone. The whole group quietly reflected, lost deep in implication.

Group assembled, sitting on stools. Emmie perched on the countertop, and he stood near enough to pick up the scent of her coconut shampoo. For a second, he studied her features as she watched the screen, long lashes casting a shadow down her cheek. Her cheeks flushed slightly, and she demurely tucked her loose hair behind her ear. Knowing he was caught, he broke his gaze.

"Wait! Stop it right there. Look at how long her fins are. She has the longer fins a body than a modern-day blue shark." Evelyn said.

"Yeah. It's huge!" agreed Alex.

"Yes, but look," said Adem approaching the monitor. "Her fins are massive compared to a Great White of comparable size. She's actually shaped a little more like a blue shark."

"What happened to her face?" asked TJ.

"There's that too," noted Dru. Her snout or rostrum is incredibly short but measuring this, she has a jaw span of about 30 feet, and in this still, I can count over 250 teeth which are about twelve to twenty inches in length."

"That's fucking terrifying," responded

Alex very unscientifically. "And it seems like she had an especially gross attitude too. Can you tell the gender?" he asked inquisitively.

"I'm not seeing a pair of claspers, a male identifier in many modern sharks." Examined Evelyn. "More importantly, can she buccal pump? If so, she won't need to be submerged to breath."

"I'm guessing so." Adem observed, "because she's already been out of the water for five minutes and doesn't seem compromised."

"She seems to be calculating." Emmie pointed out in alarm, taking a closer look.

"I'm looking at her dermal denticles." Evelyn was puzzled, honing in on the subtle color shift.

"A shark's skin, or shagreen, is like a

cat's tongue. Rough from one direction but slick from the other, which helps them slide through the water.

"Would that be hydrodynamics?" Alex asked.

"Precisely," Evelyn responded absently, still questioning whether or not those scales were changing tone.

As the film played out, demonstrating the catastrophe, the team members took turns covering their mouths and muttered obscenities. When the beast came into view, Dru paused the image, and simulated measurements were taken.

"The Infinydon is estimated to be three hundred, fifty-six feet long."

"That can't be right!" TJ said.

"That measurement is a modest estimate

overcompensating for perspective," Dru responded. The rest of the footage was watched in silence, with the group huddled together in solidarity. Paralyzed by the atrocity, Evelyn had hot tears rolling down her cheeks, facing the gravity of what they were up against, never becoming more apparent.

Adem was the first to speak once it was over. "I need a blue print of her anatomy, the best we can concoct so we can engineer a ambush."

"We have to trap her." Evelyn agreed. "I was hoping if we just raised her out of the water, nature would take its course, but she doesn't seem phased by being emersed. I wouldn't imagine she could tolerate being beached for an extended period because of her weight. Controlling her is going to be challenging.

"She has to die," Alex said, taking the last swig of his coffee and tossing the cup in the garbage in a defiant act of finality.

Dru returned from the bathroom with her kinky curls into a fresh pony tale and said, "Take a short recess. Conference Room in Ten. Team, we're going to have to kill this primordial bitch!"

After spending a few minutes regrouping, the group trickled in and saw a list of facts on the monitor that they already knew about her.

Adem began, "I would just like to say for the record, as a scientist, it only seems ethical to collect her and study her at least for a while,"

"But," Evelyn broke it, "We've

realized beyond a reasonable doubt that she's far too dangerous, and we don't have the resources to house or care for an animal as powerful and massive as she."

"So, we agree that we have to kill her?" TJ asked.

"Well, it will be her or us," Emmie said.

"Just for a moment," Alex broke in, "Let's try to think of this objectively. Is it possible that we have lived out our reign as the dominant lifeform on this planet?"

"I'll agree that we've been pretty terrible stewards of this place the last few hundred years." Evelyn resolved.

"As far as we can tell, scientifically, we've been the worst keepers this planet has ever had. We're the only species in known history to indiscriminately waste, kill each other with little to no discretion, damage our environment to the evocation of climate change, and to cause the extinction of innumerable species of flora and fauna." -TJ agreed.

"So, what are you guys saying? That maybe our time as a lifeform is over?" Emmie asked incredulously.

"I'm just saying that we have a responsibility to consider the ramifications of our situation and our actions scientifically, intelligently. We should try to remove each of ourselves from the equation and consider solutions mathematically." Adem clarified.

"If we win this war, what are the chances mankind will survive the foreseeable future in light of our destructive habits?" Evelyn examined.

"It has already been calculated and established that our earth's destruction is imminent. There is another team who's researching colonization of other planets. We are already preparing for our planet's demise as a direct result of human behavior." Dru remarked.

"So... if we win this war and live, it may only be for a brief time. Not only will we kill ourselves, but likely most other lifeforms on this planet as well." Alex acquiesced.

"Is it not too late to change?" Adem debated really not liking the turn of this conversation.

"Our behavioral change would have to be radical." Emmie rationalized. "We have overpopulated the planet. We would have to alter our way of life almost completely and go back to living off the land in harmony with nature and learn to stop taking beyond what the earth willingly gives us. Also, we would have to do away with burning fossil fuels and only use renewable energies. We would have to stop mass agriculture and using chemicals and pesticides. Of course, we would have to stop polluting and creating undue waste."

"I hate to say this, but people would never agree to do that if they have a choice." Due said. "Many people would rather stick their heads in the sand and ignorantly believe that if this situation is not going to affect them directly today, they are not willing to give up comfort to make the change."

"Tony Robbins said it best when he said that Change happens when the pain of staying the same is greater than the pain of change."

Adem affirmed. "The pain of what will happen eventually is too great for most people to even fathom."

"Yes, but, on the other hand, we must also consider that it does seem to go against our biology as the dominant life form to just lay down before our competitor even if that seems like the ethical choice? Isn't that urge to fight and kill not an integral part of our innate biology encouraging us to prevail? Isn't that a shining example of the theory of survival of the fittest? If we survive this, maybe it proves that we are intelligent lifeforms that can make progress!" Alex suggested.

"I guess," Emmie articulated, "that would be demonstrated by which species wins and where they go from there."

"May the best species win." Evelyn

declared in a somber tone. The whole group quietly reflected, lost deep in implication.

CHAPTER TWENTY FIVE

CONFESSION

BACK AT THEIR loft, Adem and Evelyn quickly walked through sweltering temperatures, relishing their domicile's dark cool. Sipping a tonic, shoes kicked off, they cuddled up on the couch, troubling thoughts on their minds but bothersome bellies growling for sustenance.

"We are both hot and tired, but I'm hungry. I have a plan," Evelyn stated, untangling herself from him on the couch.

"Wait! Where do you think you're going?" he asked of her while pulling her down to him for a kiss.

"We have some gouda, and some brie,

some turkey and salami, some Triscuits, and some Ritz crackers. I'll cut up some fruit and throw it on a charcuterie board. Voilà, dinner will be served," she offered judiciously.

"That sounds good," he agreed. "It's too hot for warm food," he said. Suddenly solemn, "I've been meaning to tell you I'm sorry for everything you went through before our separation and all of that." She turned toward him, eyeing him carefully. She looked up, timidly, curiously, and prodded.

"To what are you referring exactly?" she probed, wondering if she might receive the in-depth apology she'd been hoping for since the accident. Knowing that this conversation could get heavy quickly, she wasn't sure she had the energy for this type of exchange.

"The whole explosion in the lab and

everything that followed. You told me to slow down and follow safety protocol, but I jumped forward, and, because of my choices, you ended up hurt," he offered.

"Well," she reasoned, "I was there too. I could've reported you or something. So, it was as much my fault as yours."

"Reported me? Really? That's crap, and you know it," he said. "If I had known what could have happened, I never would have been so aggressive," he explained. Wrapping her arms around her body and lowering her head, she countered.

"But you did know. You knew that you were endangering both of us. That is why those rules are in place, to avoid injury and you went ahead without regard for yourself, me, or anyone else. We're lucky no one was killed.

Well, no one important anyway."

"No one important? Who are you talking about?"

"No one. Nothing," she bit back, regretting the remark.

"This is news. Who died?" he questioned, standing up and coming over to her. They stood chest to chest. He put his finger under her chin, lifting her face so her eyes would meet his. "Don't shut me out," he pleaded. "This is what happened before. This is why we ended up separated."

"The reason we ended up separated had nothing to do with what I did or did not do!" she clarified, shrugging his biceps off her shoulders.

"Is there someone else involved in our breakup of whom I'm not aware?" he asked, totally caught off guard.

"There was," she whispered.

"Evelyn Marie, were you…? You were seeing someone. Is that why you became so distant? Is it over, at least?" he pleaded. She stared at him, shooting icy daggers at him while he rubbed her arms. "Tell me, Darling. I'm listening."

"I can't do this tonight. I'm going to take a bath," she said, loosening from his grasp and heading upstairs, chest tightening in anxiety.

"I'll go with you," he followed her to the elegant bathroom with a large, claw-footed bathtub. She turned on the hot water tap, dropped in a lavender bath bomb, and lit a eucalyptus candle. She quickly pulled her waist-length locks into a messy topknot and turned out the bright lights. She dropped her clothes into the hamper; he followed suit.

"What are you doing?" she asked incredulously.

"I'm getting in with you to give you that back rub that you've been asking for."

"You hate baths!"

"But I love you and I need to know what happened between us. We've already wasted too much time. I have to hear this. Whatever you are going to say, I'm ready."

He stepped in the steaming water, wincing slightly at the idea of scalding his jewels, which made her crack a smile.

"Turn it down, Silly. I didn't know you were getting in." He adjusted the knobs, swished the water around, and then settled himself down. She climbed in after him and nestled herself between his tree trunks for thighs. Reluctant to relax but feeling happy enough that her mood was turning. She was pleased with how well he knew her and that he knew just what to do. Gleefully, she reached for her bath oil and dribbled it all over her shoulders. Not that stuff, he thought. Grimacing, he put his hands in the oil, disliking the feel, but he loved his wife, he reminded himself. Already soaked with oil, he began to massage, moving his hand over her glossy smooth skin, feeling for knots and tension that he could loosen and unwind tenderly. Having taken the plunge, he decided that maybe he liked the sensation of how his fingers moved with the aid of the emollient. His rough fingers glided over her supple copper skin. Getting lost in action, he rubbed both shoulders and began to work on her neck until he heard her sigh and felt the knots unbind and melt away.

"No matter what happened, I'm prepared to move past it, but I need to hear it so it no longer stands in between us," he interjected, rousing her from a steamy daze.

"Fine. You want to know?" the woman asked, realizing that if the world was ending, she might as well say her piece. "It was obviously because of the accident that I couldn't conceive. I'm broken, barren, defective."

"Conceive? We hadn't even decided to have a baby." he was utterly confounded by this turn.

"We were talking about it. I made an appointment to stop my birth control, and when I did, the doctor had some concerns. She asked if I wanted fertility testing, so I went ahead. It was determined that the radiation I was exposed to likely damaged my eggs; I was devastated." He pulled her close against his chest and held her tight at this news.

"We had started discussing it, and then you stopped talking about it. I thought you lost interest. You grew colder and more distant. I just thought that maybe you changed your mind because you were so angry with me about whatever was making you mad. We were busy. I just thought maybe you had decided against motherhood, against having a family with me."

"No. You brought it up like three more times, making plans for our future with a child. I didn't know what to say. You idiot! You thought I could lose interest in you, the ultimate love of my life? Me not want to bring a child in this world that's part you and part me? What would I not want about that?"

"I couldn't say, and I didn't want to pressure you if that was not your desire. I certainly didn't want you to have a kid for my sake."

"I knew having a child of your own would be important to you, and then you started getting all preachy with your Bible studies. When I started listening to you, it seemed that a repeated theme was how the downfall of mankind was a woman's fault and how infertility is punishment for unworthy women. It was crushing. Is that what you thought of me?"

"What? No! Why would you have thought that?"

"Because you started moving away from me and then you suddenly decided to leave the department. I thought if you couldn't have a child with me, you deserved to have a chance with someone else. So, I tried to let you go but I thought once you'd had time think about it and come back and we'd work things out. Maybe you just needed a few days to miss me." She stopped talking and turned in the water, facing each other. "Thoughts of you moving on with another woman tormented me."

"That's insane. You're crazy. You know that? Just because I am enamored with the ideas of having a little one with you, does not mean I would want to impregnate someone else. There was no reason you should have gone through all of that alone. You should have been honest with me."

"Me, crazy?" she asked, still hung up on that one word she found the ultimate insult, tears flooding down her rosy cheeks.

"Yes, Honey. Yes, but you're my crazy, and I wouldn't have it any other way. You're my beautiful, elegant, intelligent, hardworking, unique, maniac woman. You're so soft and dewy but hard as nails when you need to be, and you're always evolving and becoming better than you were before. You amaze me every day! "Let's try to make a baby," he suggested, tracing her bottom lip with his thumb and feeling his body stirring at the thought.

"We can't." she lamented.

"We can't? We can't even try?" he asked teasingly.

"Well, we can try, but we can't conceive."

"Who's to say for a fact? Right now, a mad dinosaur is planning our extinction. Who's to say what's impossible?" he asked her honestly.

"I'm deformed," she said, using her hands to cover her body. "I'm not even a woman anymore."

"I know things about you and would beg to differ," he said, letting his words slide down her spine as he made a trail of wet kisses down her neck. Having this burden off her chest and knowing that he still accepted and loved her unconditionally was all she needed to hear. She was his, all his. Her body went lax in reciprocity.

"Okay," she whispered in his ear, arms locked around his neck, steam rising from her shoulders. He took her consent without hesitation and stood lifting them both, water pouring back into the tub as if they were a ship departing the sea. Laughing, she wrapped her legs around him as he boldly stepped out of the tub, arms locked around her, water spilling haphazardly. Giggling, she held tight like a little koala bear as he slogged across the bedroom carpet and tossed her onto the bed. Seeing her skin prickle from the cold, he decided to lay over her to warm her up, his eyes dancing. Welcoming him now that he was warm and a little less drippy, she laughed as he shook his head like a dog shedding water from his hair so it wouldn't drip onto her. This bed was where they made up for the months of lost time. They made love that night and early into the morning.

CHAPTER TWENTY SIX

THE SCHIZOPHRENIC AND THE HERETIC

DELSIN PULLED OUT his earbuds, having heard a knock at the front door.

"Del!" his mother called gently as she popped her head into the bedroom. "A man is at the door for you, a priest. He said he has to talk to you." He looked up at her. "Should I tell him no?" she asked, knowing he had chosen to withdraw from the public eye.

"No, Mother. Thank you." He rose, setting down his phone. Barefooted, carpet fibers tickling his soles, he walked toward the door, always gracious of the unacquainted luxury he was now living.

"Mr. Buck!" Father Johnson said, perking with Delsin in view. The handsome caramel-skinned man approached the door and stuck his hand out in a cool greeting toward the man, his face expressionless. Chris took it, clasping it warmly in both hands, and gave it a good shake, thinking, Goodness, you could chisel ice with that jawline. "Mr. Buck, I'm Father Christopher Johnson. It is so nice to meet you. I've seen you online, and I would love to talk with you." he said, smiling. "I've emailed you a few times but not heard back." Del stopped him right there, palm up, shaking his head.

"Father, I'm not longer doing interviews and, to be honest, I am not interested in having any spiritual debates at this point."

"Oh, no! I', not here for that. I…. I'm sorry. I…" breaking eye contact, squinting, looking up, grasping for words. "How do I explain this?" he muttered. At this point, Christopher pinched his nose between two fingers and scrunched his nose.

"Mr. Buck, may I please come in?" hands steepled, droplets of sweat on his brow. Delsin sighed, having already decided to let the man in. Still, he was waiting, interested in seeing exactly how this would play out since the priest said he was not here to discuss his potential descent into hell or his need for exorcism. He stepped back, opened the door the rest of the way, and held a well-built arm out, offering an invitation. Chris nervously stepped forward and quickly noticed the view of the ocean.

"Oh! That's... Oh?" he pointed with concern in his voice, looking out at the ocean. Delsin followed his lead, walked over to the window, put his hands in his pockets, and leaned against the window. "It's... you can see that it's so much higher than it used to be." Looking at Delsin for confirmation that what he was seeing was accurate."

"Mm-hmm." Delsin agreed. Both men looked out over the rooftops of the lower buildings at the beachfront properties and businesses which were now underwater. Angry waves violently crashed up, depositing sand onto the previously busy avenues. Meteorologists predicted that water levels would rise exponentially as the full moon approached. Chris put a hand up to his mouth when he noticed the carrion of lifeless marine creatures of countless species. Jellyfish, swordfish, and porpoises washed ashore, littering the streets like garbage. There were vast sections of fractured coral with the jagged remains erupting from the sand.

"I've stayed away from the water because…Well, you know. She's out there." Chris told the young man. Delsin nodded thoughtfully. "Are you? Do you? I mean, I've watched several videos but what I see seems different from what you see." Chris said, grappling to find the words.

"What do you see?" Delsin asked, his interest piqued. He had yet to encounter anyone who might be sharing this experience with him. Delsin sat back in an armchair and motioned for Chris to sit across from him. His mother entered, bringing each man a glass of water. "Father, this is my mother, Mary.

"My son is gifted by being able to commune with the Great Spirits. Do you speak with your god?" she asked of the priest earnestly as she perched on the sofa's edge.

"Well, maybe. I really don't know

or understand what's been happening to me. At first, I thought I had a brain tumor, but it seems I don't. Then, I thought I must be schizophrenic, but when I realized that I was seeing events that were actually happening, I knew that what I was experiencing was real. Although related, it doesn't seem to be the same thing you are experiencing. Delsin and his mother looked at one another, unsure what to make of this peculiar sweaty man. Chris began to laugh as he vocalized his explanation. "I actually... became her."

"Okay. So, you are the monster? You are the one doing all of this damage?" she asked, attempting to cover her amusement with the heel of her hand

and putting her glass down.

"Mother!" Del reprimanded amiably. "I'm sorry."" He said to the priest. "Can you explain anymore?"

"So…" stammering and then chuckling in embarrassment, he cleared his throat and extrapolated. "I don't think that I'm a shark. I… am, a man, to be sure, however, there are times when I go into this seizure-like-trance where I see through the eyes of the beast. I have been with her all along from the time her release." Delsin looked up at his sister at the term release, who had wandered into this common room. That was a part of the story he had not been privy to, and he was trying to determine the validity of this man's account. His sister had emerged as her curiosity had been stirred upon hearing an unfamiliar voice. The only guest they'd had since they came here was Gideon. When her brother looked up at her, she shrugged lightly to say she didn't currently hold an opinion but needed to hear more. She silently settled herself in the same room but in adjacent seating as if not to impose, indicating she was listening but did not want to participate. She began to sketch, appearing disinterested, but it was evident that she attended as an audience supporting her brother. She knew he'd been treated unkindly since they'd last lived together, and she needed him to know that even though she didn't quite understand what was happening, she wished to advocate for him however possible.

The sun traveled the arc of the stratosphere as the priest told the family all that he knew from beginning to end.

CHAPTER TWENTY SEVEN

VANGUARD

ONCE THE PLAN had been devised, the team was given a seven-day sabbatical. Supplies would be gathered in their absence, and travel plans readied. They were ordered to go and spend time doing whatever they wished with whomever they chose with strong consideration to the probability that their plan may fail. Michaels released them from their current contracts giving the following directive:

"*Half of life is lost in charming others. The other half is lost in going through anxieties caused by others. Leave this play. You have played enough.* -Rumi. Have fun, People. You have each been paid a sum of 500 million dollars. Additionally, you will be provided any transportation for travel to anywhere you desire and have been given legal immunity for any petty crimes committed while on leave. I request that you not murder unnecessarily or share our government's secret; ultimately, the choice is yours. Do what you will, and I would ask to see you back in 168 hours." The group was astounded by this announcement but quickly found their voices to begin stating their requests, each with a unique journey in mind.

Twenty Hours Later

The world's most prominent international leaders sat in a Global Crisis Intervention Assembly in London. Wide eyed they watched an assemblage of facts captioning the calamity, a compilation of footage that illustrated worldwide decimation. Statistics flashed across the screen representing the rising international death toll on an enormous monitor. Afterward, they were pummeled with a barrage of the predicted implications proposed by their scientific teams from the differing nations.

"We've made two significant failed attempts to killed this beast, and now we've discovered that there are actually two of them," said Prime Minister of Spain Cabrera.

"We could be facing extinction if we don't work together on this one." stated US Madame President Taylor.

"I am prepared to nuke them," said Great Leader Yang of North Korea.

"And kill us all? That may not be necessary. Our research indicates that they can be isolated and killed." said French President Evans.

"We must track both animals and plan a simultaneous attack as they seem to be communicating," added Spain's Prime Minister Cabrera.

"They must die." Agreed, President of Brazil Batista.

"We can use atomic bombs." suggested Indonesia President Kusuma. After another few hours of futile discussion, the panel voted unanimously to attempt cryogenic freezing and to detonate two neutron bombs as a failsafe once they could track them sufficiently. This needed to be orchestrated so the two would surface around the full moon as the tides flooded the beaches utilizing beacons to lure them and radar to track them.

Returning to their respective nations upon the conclusion of the meeting, they began focusing on monitoring the beasts in a collaborative effort to deliver the world's last living dinosaurs to their final destination.

The American team was scheduled to report on Monday so the plan could be set in motion. A prep team was packed up and headed abroad to a crudely salvaged marine base near the Banda Arc off the Coast of Indonesia, tasked with constructing the towers needed to set their plan in motion.

CHAPTER TWENTY EIGHT

ALEXANDER

ALEX WAS THE first to act. He wasted no time contacting his potential love interest, a woman named Xanthie, from his home office. He phoned her offering her a week-long visit to Paris, the City of Love; however, Alex had chosen to keep the roiling sore a secret to allow for a carefree weekend with his impromptu date. She delightedly took him up on his offer. Better late than never was the theme of her response, asking what took him so long. Within hours, they were whisked overseas in a private jet.

Once they landed, had unpacked, and rested for a few hours, they ventured to The

Butte Montmartre, home of artists, musicians, dancers, and old films. They partook in the architecture of the Sacré-Coeur, enjoying the views.

"Montmartre's charm lies in its history," he drawled as they walked lazily next to one another like familiar lovers. Smiling, observing the city of the Belle Epoque, the interesting people, the charming little cafes, and quaint shops. They wandered in and out of tiny brasseries tasting deserts, sipping espresso, and getting lost in the atmosphere.

On the second day, they traced the loving engravings on The Wall of Love tucked away in Jehan Rictus Square, hundreds of professions of love written in countless languages. Lingering, they explored the tranquil garden of the Museum of Romantic

Life. They crossed The Pont des Arts, the Love Lock Bridge, and left their own padlock behind as a tangible exclamation of their present emotion. They discussed their first impressions of each other, and she probed deeper into why he'd waited so long to make his move.

They were allowed into the Place Dauphine with little governmental interference. They lingered in the Square du Vert Galant, where they enjoyed crystalline waters where he stole a kiss or two, surrounded by the sophisticated verdure of the gardens. That night, they sipped coffee sheltered from the drizzle from the awning from their hotel balcony, cuddled up under a blanket, watching barges peacefully floating passed gulls calling in the distance, noting the rising water levels, but things were peaceful here otherwise.

Their favorite place to visit throughout the week was the Parc Montsouris. They found a quiet bench near the waterside, where they relaxed in the shade. Unzipping his pack, he tossed a blanket onto the lush grass and sat down, folding his legs and patting the ground. He invited her to join him. Delighted by this sweet surprise, she kicked off her shoes. She closed her eyes, toes sinking into the lush cool grass, taking note of the sensation. Flipping back through her memory book of perceptions, she couldn't recall having this feeling since she was a kid. Taking her time, consciously enjoying the feeling on her soles, she joined him in the dappled shade. He laid back, encouraging her to follow suit. She laid one forearm over her eyes for shade, relaxing fully with her companion.

"Have you decided that I am not going to murder you yet?" he asked her in good humor, them being relatively new acquaintances.

"I have," she responded without any hesitation.

"So, you agreed to travel abroad with me before you knew? A woman can never be too careful these days…" he chided.

"Yes, you passed my test the third time I met you almost a year ago."

"You've been testing me?"

"I have!" she confessed. "I mean, how could I agree to a proposal of marriage from someone who may be a serial killer," she asked of him. At this, he bolted upright.

"Marriage? What? When did this thought enter your mind?"

"Thought? This is not mere fantasy. I'm a statistician. It's a prediction based on the facts of your behavior. You've been wanting to ask me out since the Geneva meeting but chickened out after you saw me accept a date from someone else. You were taking too long so I decided to force your hand by presenting a rival but you backed off. Then were finally going to ask me out on your last trip last month but then you got whisked away on some secret mission," she explained.

"Damn. You've got it all figured out," he mused.

"Well, I don't know where you've been or what you've been up but it's serious because you haven't relaxed this whole time regardless of how charming I am and how innately comfortable we have been together. Plus, I'm hot as hell. I mean, all your dreams have come true here and there you are worrying about… whatever."

"Yeah. I have been a little tense. Sorry about that," he said, rolling over. He propped himself up on one elbow to face her.

"So, when was this wedding going to take place?" he asked in utter confusion.

"Well, we're not super young but I still need to put you through the paces to make sure you can keep up with me, so we were going to date for nine months and then be engaged for a year but that was twelve months ago. So, you're running behind schedule. They way I see it now, you have six months to court me and then pop the question. It doesn't have to all be trips abroad, but I'll need some excitement because we will slow down and have two kids before I'm thirty-two and I'm nearly thirty." At this, he raised his eyebrows, sucked a deep breath in, and laid back, closing his eyes.

"Okay!" Apparently, I didn't surprise you."

"Yes, and we're going to have a long, mostly happy marriage and you're going to probably have a heart attack and die despite staying fit and healthy when you're sixty-three or so." At this, his eyes popped open. "Yes, I hacked your family's medical history, but I'll still live to my nineties. So, I'm going to date as a widow and likely remarry, which our daughters will support because I was a dutiful wife to be. They will be strong independent women who understand that I deserve happiness."

"Really?" he sat up, studying her expression. She pulled her arm away from her face, locking eyes with him, and then erupted with laughter at the look on his face.

"Are you going to kiss me or what?" she finally asked point-blank. Swooping in, he cut her off by grazing his lips over hers. Reaching her arms around his neck and pulling him down to her breast, with some coaxing, she allowed him to kiss her deeply. When the couple came up for air, she was giggling.

"Finally, you relaxed!" she remarked.

"Well, why do I need to worry about anything when you have it all figured out?" he asked.

"You don't," she responded confidently.

"Okay, then," he acquiesced, genuinely gladdened by the idea but also sad. He laid back down next to her.

"So, tell me about our kids," he urged, one silent tear rolling down his cheek, which she missed. Her eyes skyward, she watched the clouds as she described the children who would never come to fruition because he reflected this woman and all women and all men, for that matter, were not very long for this world.

"Well, we'll have two girls, eighteen months apart, Maia and Morgan, and they'll be beautiful and smart. I mean look at us. They will have hit the jackpot. They will be the apple of your dad's eye and like second kids to my parents. My parents are younger than your dad, she pointed out. I know your mother is already gone. I am sorry for that," she whispered, squeezing his hand. She went on animatedly for several minutes, lost in the manifestation of her future. Projections for her future with this man of her whom she had yet to technically claim as her own. As the sun softened, the two fell asleep in each other's arms, shadows traveling across their bodies as the afternoon expired, one day closer to potential doom.

The following day they lay in bed and ordered room service, touring each other's childhoods and discovering surprising things about each other. He used to sing in a heavy metal band. That made her laugh heartily, teasing him about all of the women with whom he likely dallied. Rested, they dressed, ate a sumptuous lunch downstairs, and then visited a traditional English garden with primeval trees, ponds, and waterfalls. Here is where he learned about her education abroad, as well as more of her hopes for the future she was certain was ahead of them. As knowledgeable as she was, she was not privy to the fate which lay ahead.

Atop a horse-drawn carriage, they reconnoitered sundry gardens and museums. They dined lazily on the Seine River and enjoyed the architecture of Le Meurice. They took a walking tour of the Montmartre, whispering secrets while feeding each other the most delectable crème caramel. As the moon rose and the world turned, he chose to live in the moment. They were safe for now, tucked sweetly inside their hotel. They bathed and surveyed each other's warmth, tenderly tumbling between cool flax linen.

CHAPTER TWENTY EIGHT

NOMADS

EMMIE ASKED TJ if he would spend his week with her. He responded that wild horses couldn't drag him away from her. She leaped when he suggested that they go to Greece. They had gotten to know each other well and discovered they shared the enthusiasm for travel. After being spirited away, the couple checked into their room and excitedly explored the hotel as they discussed the esoteric architectural features they noticed up and down the halls. Their hotel looked like a historical building. Every hallway and piece of furniture looking to belong in a museum. It made them feel as if they were living in another time, one less perilous. They wasted no time tossing their bags into the room and striking out into the moonlit night. They walked the streets side-by-side, pointing and talking as they observed the charming details of the city.

Smells of spices, fresh fruits, and coffee from the warmly lit buildings and taverns piqued their appetite. Suddenly realizing they were famished, they wandered into a café and ordered whatever the waitress recommended, not even asking what it was. Tension ebbed as they grazed on the basket of Spanakopita. Emmie picked up a triangle of warm, buttery, flaky phyllo filled with feta, dill, and cooked spinach. Her cheeks puckered at the zest of lemon. TJ leaned forward, opening his beak like a baby bird. She stuffed an enormous piece in his mouth, tittering. He closed his eyes laughing, relishing the vignette of tastes. They thoroughly enjoyed the exotic fragrances of their meal as they sipped rick aromatic drinks and conversed intensely as the evening turned deep into the night. They were pleasantly surprised at the savory piquancy as they explored their meals and nibbled off of each other's plates comfortably.

They studied the other raptly. Emmie caught herself smiling at his bushy expressive eyebrows. He animated tales about his childhood, describing his antics in school, sharing stories of life with his parents and siblings, living in an underdeveloped county in humble conditions, and all about his ragtag gang of friends. Emmie winced as he described things about his brother, who had just passed. That explained that Jasir being gone didn't yet feel like reality. He was still in shock over it, which he was willing to allow for the time being. Surprisingly, she discovered he'd had a short career as a pilot in Saudi Arabia. He, in turn, enjoyed the flourish of her long delicate fingers as she recounted her childhood chronicles. She illustrated tales of her past in which her father taught her how to woodwork. How they built a deck one winter and assembled custom furniture in the summertime. TJ searched her face trying to decide if she was jesting when she told him about the time she watched in horror as her strong-as-an-ox father drilled through his finger with a power tool but didn't stop building the staircase he was working on. The man only asked her for a headlamp as the sun had already gone down, and he could obviously no longer see. Emmie went on to say that her grandfather, the carpenter, had cut his pointer finger off years back and treated it just about as nonchalantly.

"Off," was the only question asked.

"Off," she clarified. "He picked it up, wrapped his bloody stump in a dusty shop towel, and put the digit in his pocket so he could keep working." So, a drill through the finger was considered a minimal affair among the men in her family. TJ was genuinely uncertain what to make of that story. Barbarians was his initial thought. Admirable legends of her heroic father soon morphed into tender memories of being curled up next to her mother, lovingly reading children's narratives of a boy and his Pooh bear, a good dog named Carl, and fantastical fairy tales from generations past. She repeated comical stories of beloved pets and the sacred places she once played. He was mesmerized by the shapely curve of her lips, her finely knit brows, and the shimmer in her glossy eyes as she became somewhat emotional at the remembrance. These memories were bittersweet with the realization that the extinction of her whole family was imminent if they did not soon succeed. They ended the night soaking in the private hot tub outside their room, the crisp nocturnal air caressing and teasing their bare flesh.

The following morning, the two hailed a taxi at dawn and began adventuring. They hiked to the great St. Stephen monastery in the Meteora, which appeared artfully frozen in time. This was the only monastery visible from

Kalambaka and had been a place of pilgrimage for almost 10,000 years. This sacred location has a long history of miracles, and so it was here that the two knelt in meditative prayer. They prayed for success once the plan went into action. They begged for the preservation of their species. They pled for their families' well-being and asked for wisdom and peace of mind if these days or weeks were to be their final moments. The monks posted there in meditation spoke of the two in Hellēniké, remarking on their youth, positive energy, and divine fate to have fallen in love during such a dire time. A third man joined them as the trio walked away, in their divine knowledge debating in their native tongue whether or not it was a good time for mankind to die off.

"It's been too long, and man has done a

poor job. It is time for our planet to enjoy cleansing and rebirth," the tallest one argued. After a circular debate, they all essentially agreed with him. This structure had seen thousands of men come before these two. This ancient monastery no longer shone as it had in its former glory. It had been defaced throughout multiple wars. In its golden years, it served as a nunnery and ultimately a museum hosting the display of ancient reliquiae and trinkets from another time.

Two days later, they stood breathlessly in the ancient Temple of Poseidon, holding each other as she shed tears of awe, the warm breeze from the ocean teasing. He watched her in smoldering fascination. As they explored, she ran her hands over antediluvian relics. In Skala Erresos, they played sweet games in the town square with the locals, just like children. They stuffed their bellies taut with foreign delicacies in the charming village of Chalki, a place world away from anything else. Fortunately, in these most remote areas, the crisis hadn't affected them yet, and these little villages appeared oblivious of the ticking time bomb that was preparing to explode. The next night, in the magic of the Naxos countryside, they finally consummated their nascent liaison. From then on, they stayed within the walls of their hotel, content on an exploration of the heart rather than the world.

CHAPTER TWENTY NINE

DRU

DRU TOOK A direct flight from DC to her family home in North Carolina. At the airport, she ran straight into the arms of her anxious boyfriend. She broke into a run as soon as she spotted him in the terminal. He instinctively wrapped his arms around her protectively, crooning.

"Carwyn!" she cried.

"Sweetheart?" he embraced her strongly with brawny arms, happy to see her but perplexed at her upset. She was often a frustratingly pragmatic young woman. He'd never seen her less than level-headed in public in all their years. She often chose the path of logic in the face of heated disagreement. When she was selected to work on this team, the initial part of the assignment was a confidentiality agreement, stacks of contracts enclosed with red tape surmounted by threats of imprisonment in the case of a potential breach. For this reason, he was oblivious of the top-secret project she'd been working on.

Now that she was home, circumstances had changed. Upon her return, Dru called her immediate family together, along with Carwyn, and shared the dire news. She began by simply stating that she had life-threatening information to share. Taking her time, she first told them about each team member with whom she'd been working. Laughing, she described each with their distinctions and idiosyncrasies, Anton being the most eccentric and peculiar. TJ, the young foreign geologist. Alex, the handsome but morose businessman. Emmie is the elegant and hardworking biology researcher. The married scientists were romantic goals in her book; they were a perfectly complementary pair and so bright. After delving into the intense level of secrecy and how she met each of her colleagues, she digressed by describing every preemptive thought that had ever entered her beautiful head. Tucked safely in her parents' lodge, they all sat stricken with suspense, maddened by wondering what menace was threatening their firstborn child.

Finally, gathering curly locks nervously behind her ears, with one of Carwyn's hands on her shoulder for support, she narrated the lengthy account of all the cadre had learned.

She wept as she recounted the gruesome genocide she had witnessed and paraphrased the projections of the predicted events. Everyone sat in silence with gazes fixed. They looked at each other for clues as to how to react; Carwyn grabbed Dru and held her tightly as she sobbed fitfully. She wore herself out. From his slouched position on the couch, her little brother began texting, seaming unphased. Her father stood and began pacing, asking ridiculous questions while her mother spun her ring in her hand. Feeling weak, her mother laid her head in her hands and began to rock quietly, wiping teardrops from her rosy cheeks. The next hour was spent answering unanswerable questions in a firing range manner. Finally, her little brother was overcome with boredom at the logistics and interjected, shifting the entire mood.

"D, you're saying the world is ending, like, soon?"

"Yes." She answered, squared-shouldered, not bothering to mince words.

"So... YOLO. I mean, let's do whatever we want," he suggested, simply looking around the room at the dramatic upheaval. Family members examining each other, and they essentially agreed. Her father shrugged and began cooking an authentic Indian dinner. Her mother blew her nose, loosening her shoulders in resignation. Dru was shocked at the idea. She was wholly committed to a grievous dismal reunion with her loved ones and a depressing last few days. She had already decided not to bear the burden alone, regardless of the circumstances.

"Dru," Carwyn interrupted, holding her hand and getting down on one knee, "Will you do me the honor of..."

"Yes!" She shrieked, jumping off of the couch and toppling him backward. "Let's get married!"

Her mother turned, mouth hanging by this unexpected turn of events.

"We are going to begin planning a wedding this week?" her father inquired, smiling, as the ingredients in his cookware began to steam, filling the room with tantalizing fragrances.

"Tomorrow." She announced matter-of-factly. "We are getting married tomorrow." Dialing Michaels, she made a few calls. The Pentagon will have it all arranged.

When in private with her fiancé, she

apologized for the times when she was difficult or placed her journey ahead of her his. She professed her true heart, explaining that she didn't always feel brave and calm but thought that she had something to prove and therefore felt that she must. Next, she demanded to be comforted and caressed while they still had time. Early the following day, one phone call putting a wedding into place by the president's mandate at six that evening. Without a worry, she took a long luxurious bath, wondering how beautiful her wedding gown would be. A wedding, a honeymoon, all in the next few days, brief though they were likely to be. Although intentionally joyous, the events were overshadowed by the bereavement of what may soon come.

Come evening, she found herself

walking on her father's arm down a gravel path in between rustic chairs filled with the faces of every person she'd ever known and loved in Hawkesdene Estate in Andrews, North Carolina. The lush aromatic bouquets of lilies and roses scented the grounds. She was wrapped in a magnificent dress with an ivory gown that boasted a sheer lace bodice and a plunging off-the-shoulder neckline. It glimmered from every angle with sequin, pearls, and beads, highlighting her slim but healthy silhouette. Everyone stood revered as she floated down the aisle, displaying the couture low-backed gown with silk-covered buttons, a V-pattern that echoed the chapel-length train.

The father kissed the bride and gave her away, the toe-headed ring bearer produced the ring, the candles were lit, and the sweethearts made their claims and proclamations of all they would do for their entire lives, whether that be one week or one century. The trees high above them created a shady canopy leaves trembled, whispering well wishes to the young couple as they said 'I do .' They kissed fervently as they were pronounced man and wife, and the pastor presented the exquisite couple. The spellbound audience stood erupting with applause, moved by the magic that hung in the air.

Through glimmering eyes, Dru gazed into the audience, tears threatening to spoil her flawless makeup. She took a deep breath and smiled at the crowd of witnesses picking out her favorites: Grandma Dot, Aunt Sue, Bea and Rover, and all the cousins with whom she grew up, as well as her closest college friends. Even her brother was clapping and smirking his approval of this milestone. When she looked more carefully, she realized he was gawking amorously upon the ample cleavage of her maid of honor which made her laugh at the poor kid.

That night the newlyweds tried to absorb every memory of the festivities as the moments ticked on. A band played while the guests dined and danced on the terrace. They chuckled as the flower girl cut across the dance floor, chasing the ring bearer with a sparkler. He shrieked with laughter, golden ringlets flying as he galloped passed, tapping in his black patent dress shoes, upsetting the purse of one older woman who was nibbling cake at her table.

As the sun fell, torches were lit, and fairy lights twinkled. It was enchanting. The warm air and exquisite venue were enough to make a bride feel as if this night was the beginning of beautiful things to come. She tried hard not to think of what may come. After a few hours, the moon rose, and the bride and groom stole away to walk the path down to the dock.

"Are you okay walking these planks in those crazy shoes," he asked tenderly, concern for his new wife, not wanting to break her the first moment he'd relinquished her from her parents. She pulled her skirts up, chuckling as she wriggled toes at the end of a bare foot. "When did that happen." he asked in dubiety. "I thought the shoes were like the crowning jewel of the dress," he rationed.

"They were," she smiled, hopping down

the steps toward the lakeside double-footed and fancy-free. "Which is why I wore them through the whole wedding and took them off the second the last ceremony photo was taken. Twirling. "You didn't even notice that I was six inches shorter when we were dancing," she pointed out.

"Well, you were regular size. So, I guess I completely forgot about the shoes," he realized.

"And so did everyone!" she craftily pointed out, grinning. "My love?" she queried, her voice turning husky.

"Yes, Kitten?" he replied, reaching for her in the dark, suddenly feeling serious.

"Did you marry just because the world is ending?"

"Not even a little bit," he stated dutifully.

"I wanted cake," he explained.

"What?" she snorted.

"Not just any cake, though. Like, a bakery-quality gourmet cake that was made for a once-in-a-lifetime event with baby blue icing. Pastels taste better than any other color. I'm not sure why." He paused mid-diatribe to see why she wasn't protesting. He looked down at her with her hands on her hips, eyes glimmering, trembling lips. "I'm kidding!" he assured, grappling her in a rough cuddling hug, and she began to bawl.

"I know you are." she sobbed. "You're just so damn silly!" she resolved. "No matter what, you always know how to counter my seriousness and lighten the mood. You are my helpmate, ally, best friend, teammate, confidant, match, and soul mate. Carwyn

Connor Kelly, you are my everything, and I am so honored to have become your wife," she said, sniffing.

"Well, yeah," he responded by simply reassuring her in his perfect way.

"Can we go to bed now? I'm suddenly very, very tired." He pulled her close, kissed her slightly damp forehead, and nodded. With that, the husband and wife left the reception together without saying goodnight and retired to their rapturous honeymoon suite, from which they did not emerge until late afternoon the next day. It was a good choice if this night had to be one of their last.

CHAPTER THIRTY

THE DOCS

ADEM AND EVELYN were immediately airborne, returning to their cozy abode off the California coast. Upon arrival, they were inundated by the overwhelmingly welcome scent of the forest and the sea; they were also met with a very excited Kanik barking enthusiastically at the gate on the leash of a very annoyed driver.

The couple took him back from his driver, getting nearly knocked backward by big dog hugs. Adem picked him up and deftly set the massive malamute over his right shoulder as he mounted the stairs two by two. This act of balance and strength stirred her admiration for him. The dog-sitter shook his head bemused as he got into his car, leaving with a million-dollar tip.

When the father and son entered the house, the man deftly flipped the dog upside down on his back and cradled him like a baby asking him if he was a stinky boy while daddy was away. Kanik howled, chuffed, and groaned, recounting every painful detail of his owners' time away. Evelyn watched the dramatic scene unfold, tearful at the reunion as she ruffled the dog's belly fluff. She buried her face in his mane and opened her arms to embrace the two. She mewled gently at realizing the time she had wasted over the last months of separation. Over what? Petty grudges. At this time, she only wished to push past the regret and fill her heart with unadulterated joy at their reunion.

"What's this?" Adem inquired, smiling as he squeezed the massive dog between him and his mate so he could balance the dog while reaching one arm around his quietly sobbing wife.

"I just... I'm so sorry," she said between racking breaths.

"Sorry? For missing our dog, our only child?" he joked good-naturedly.

"A child? It really wasn't your fault that we never conceived. I don't know if that had anything to do with my infertility. I've blamed you all this time but the truth is, there was plenty of time long before that. I mean, it's a wonder I didn't get pregnant in college."

"Now? That's what you're worried about now? With the state of the world, maybe it's a blessing that we never had a kid. How would we be able to focus on the problem at hand if we were worried about the welfare of our child or children?" he asked pragmatically.

"I guess... maybe." She agreed logically. "But all of this time, I told myself that you were to blame and I worried that you would feel unfulfilled tethered to some wasteland of a woman. I worried that you wouldn't be satisfied for your whole life with just me. How could you want to grow old with a defective partner?"

"Defective?" he asked, pulling away from her, letting Kanik slide down to the floor, and taking her face in both hands as he often did. "Who's to say that our lack of children isn't my problem and what would make you think I would ever need more than we already have?" he asked sensibly. Cocking one eyebrow seriously, "and if all of this insanity has been running through your mind the last year, why haven't we been talking about it?" She lowered her eyes, considering the ramifications of her behavior. "Hmmm?" he probed lovingly.

"Forgive me?" she murmured into his shoulder.

"Only, if you can forgive me for not realizing what you've been going through. And... for my arrogance," he added. She trembled, left shaken by his love, understanding, and pure devotion.

"How?" she asked him, gazing into his eyes.

"How, what?" he inquired, a smile quirking his lips.

"How..." She let go of him and spun around their kitchen with arms raised overhead, "did I become so lucky?" Merrily, hair flying, she whirled back into his arms. "You truly are my soulmate, and if the world is going to end, I'm glad to be with you, and I want to make the best of our last days together." Kanik frolicked on his hind legs, still celebrating their reunion.

"Let's not talk about what may come. Let's just... spend time together," he suggested.

"Yes. Let's," she agreed, happily embracing a peace she had not experienced in too long. As evening sprawled gently around them, they chose to order dinner from their favorite Brazilian grill. It was delivered in record time by two unnamed FBI agents.

Relishing, they opened the containers. The savory steam wafting enticed them to dig in with abandon. While they stuffed themselves, Adem looked after his wife lovingly. They ate. She imbibed spirits. They danced to their old records wrapped only in knitted blankets, with Kanik playing along and howling his own rendition of each song. The jovial threesome ended the evening breathing deeply of cool crisp air while stargazing from the upper deck. They stayed outside, darkness gently cloaking them until the chill sent them indoors and upstairs into their bedroom. They fell into bed together with Kanik crushingly close. He felt the need to touch them both after their long separation. Soon enough, the silly dog was snoring and whining in his sleep, his feet thrumming gently as he dreamt of fast furry things skittering just out of reach.

Hours later, the sun gently roused them from their intertwined slumber. The lovers awoke stretching, bathed, and wandered downstairs for a simple breakfast. Kanik let himself out for his morning duel of red squirrels. As morning became light, they flirted, teased, and taunted each other just like they had in years past, nibbling on toast and sipping hot drinks. Breakfast culminated in a frolic atop the kitchen island, after which they both ended up ravenous for food yet emotionally satisfied. After a proper breakfast prepared in cooperation, they took a winding walk down the path from their cabin into the forest with no plan in mind. They huffed hand-in-hand with their breath puffing out like clouds while the trail was wide, Kanik contentedly marking the pass along the way. As the trail curved around the hill and narrowed, Adem instinctively took the lead. The three traveled upward. He waited patiently while his beloved stopped to sketch the different shapes of leaves and trees, illustrating the myriad of greens in an attempt to capture all of the textures and fibers of the wood. Amused, he took notice of her pausing just around the time lactic acid began to really burn in his muscles from the intensive uphill climb. His mouth quirked in observation of her gathering the pine cones along the way, but only those which she found exceptional. To him, they looked identical, but she delightedly squirreled them away in her pack, grinning at her treasure trove. When it was bursting full, he turned her around, pulled the bag from her shoulders, and took on the weight himself mainly as a tender, that's enough.

The forest floor became pleasantly warm as the sun rose and burned off the morning fog. Having reached a small summit, he was overcome with affection watching her as she tilted her head back, squinting, looking, trying to find which birds were calling. The woman perched atop a large rock and unzipped her jacket. Just as they had become damp with sweat, they reached the water's edge of the large pond. With no discussion except one cheeky look of agreement, the couple stripped out of their clothes, abandoning them on tree branches, and skinny-dipped in the crisp, calm lake. They splashed, wrestled, and squealed playfully in the clear water. Half-heartedly, the wolf-dog dawdled at the water's edge, fishing minnows and blowing bubbles with his snout. He soon found a pebbled area to sit and watch his owners with one ear cocked in the sphinx pose, diligently scouring the pads of his feet. He expertly extracted small burs from the thick fur between his toes with teeth bared. When the couple tired, they sunbathed bare-skinned on a wide, sun-kissed boulder, eventually dozing next to each other. Awoken when the sun was high in the sky, they were dry and snickered as they peeled their saliferous skin from the toasty rocks taking note of the damp impressions left behind by their bodies. They stood back, critiquing each other's soggy impressions. She complimented him on the wingspan of his shoulders, an attribute of his that she'd always found attractive. He praised her for her ample heart-shaped imprint and the dainty footprints that traveled from her resting area back into the water. Reclad somewhat haphazardly, they ventured effortlessly back down the hill.

When they reached home again, they were starving. Fish and vegetables were delivered fresh from the market with one quick call. Adem grilled as Evelyn painted on an easel out on the terrace, wearing nothing more than his worn T-shirt. Once, she gripped the collar and drank in the scent of him, his essence thick on the t-shirt he'd dampened with his pheromone-drenched perspiration. As the sun set, he guessed at the species of native plants that had begun to take shape on her canvas, inspired by the aerial view of the forest from their porch. They ate their fill and wandered up to bed early in the spirit of enjoying a quiet evening together.

As she undressed, he opened every bedroom window at her request. Snuggled together, covered in plush down, they unwound. Assuming their sleeping position: her cheek against his brawny chest, delicate shoulder tucked warmly under his virile wing with their legs intertwined, she succumbed to slumber. As the night deepened, they were lulled by the wind rustlings of the leaves, the night's song. She drowsed gently like a tiny bird. He remained awake, stroking her hair as he listened to her breath, slow and calm: steady and rhythmic. He contemplated his accomplishments, goals, dreams, those accomplished, and others he'd forgotten throughout his lifetime. An unexpected tear fell down his cheek, and he decided that he had lived his life well for the most part. His parents were proud of him. He'd positively impacted his students and was faithfully loved by an exquisite, dynamic, tiger-hearted scholar whose passion burned brightly enough to match his own. Although he didn't have any offspring to ensure his lineage, his species may soon become extinct. So, not having to concern themselves with children at this time really was a good thing. As the veil of slumber overtook him, he decided that he had no regrets and that if it could all be done again, which it could not, he would do it just the same except maybe with more patience. He and this woman, they'd made a beautiful life.

They slept late the next day and spent an idle morning indoors, only half-dressed, reminiscing about their favorite memories passed. They borrowed an Appaloosa quarter horse and a palomino Friesian from a neighbor in the afternoon. They rode horseback on the coast until dusk when they sat around a fire, poking the coals of the beach bonfire until they were sleepy.

On the last full day in their haven, they copied photographs, gathered memorabilia, wrote bits of their memoirs, recorded their final wishes in journals, and put them in a time capsule. The four federal agents charged with digging the hole were less than charmed by the task, making the project even better. Lastly, they stayed awake all night erotically tormenting each other in every room of the house, laughing, moaning, and quaking, finally reaching a zenith they had never before achieved. They worshipped each other in concert as if this night was their last. Over these days at home, they said goodbye with their bodies but never with their words, deliberate not to take any motions to tip the scale of fate against them.

The morning they were scheduled to report, they convened for a languid breakfast of fruits and pastries on the balcony, which they found on the porch after Kanik woke them barking. They stayed there scantily clad until their escorts pulled up the drive and began to badger the two by insisting, they were behind schedule and that their chopper was waiting. When the lead agent finally tossed a rock with a note atop the balcony announcing they were preparing to contact Michaels, they wandered indoors to dress and grab their bag.

CHAPTER THIRTY ONE

BANDA ARC

ON A WINDY Monday morning, the plan was set in motion. The team had returned and flown abroad to a crudely salvaged marine base on the Banda Arc off the Coast of Indonesia. A strange hybrid of optimism and dread besieged the friends equipped with their plans. They were in the air for several hours. Satellite studies showed increased activity in the region, which seemed an optimum location to erect their snare. Having been away the last week, they were somewhat recharged and ready to tackle the giantess post respite.

As they rode, they listened on headsets to sound bytes from Anton expressing accelerated concern over rising temps, mounting water levels, and the accumulating acidity of the water. Hellish freak storms were aswirl, causing unprecedented disasters on every continent. There were accounts in Mexico where citizens were being pummeled to death by basketball-sized hail. Tornados, hurricanes, and earthquakes plagued the United States; floods and mudslides afflicted Germany. Volcanos were erupting in Russia and Iceland. South China lost thousands after being surprised by freezing cyclones. Snow fell in the jungles of Brazil, and the arctics were sinking under warming water. The oceans flowed over the coasts, and vengeful winds shrieked across the landscape, uprooting farmland. Mother Nature was leaving a malevolent trail of destruction along the way.

Upon touch down, they were dropped off hastily onto the helipad. The sea spattered them as the wind tore angrily at them. They could see military teams assembling guns and catapults with sedatives and caging. They were hurried off of the aircraft, water licking at their heels.

"The pilots said they could only land here unless the pad was still above water and, as you can see, the water is rising." Michaels yelled over the turbines. Evelyn and Adem looked at each other, dismay apparent. "How we escape from here sounds will hopefully be a problem for another day," he rebutted after noting their expressions. This idea made Evie's chest tight with anxiety in conjunction with the rocky copter ride. With intention, she set the concern out of her foremind, knowing they may or may not have a tomorrow. They escaped the noise of the aircraft as it rose from its perch and followed the pandemonium of trucks and generators to the job site. The group found the two lead officials already deep in discussion. They were pointed in their tent's direction and told to put their bags down and boots on.

Dru entered their fort with a handful of Styrofoam cups and some hot cocoa mix as dusk fell. This was the best I could do. The crew was troubleshooting at two card tables, with the wind whipping around their tent seeming to impersonate their distress.

"What about the trance that sharks are supposed to enter when turned upside down?" Emmie asked. "Is that myth?"

"No. That's been proven but this species

is unique from other currently living animals in so many ways that we can't count on anything that we think we know." Adem answered.

"So, the meg... infinydon, has been dormant for the last what billion years?" TJ asked.

"Mmm... let's say 2.5 to 3.6 million or so." Evelyn conjectured, raising her voice over the ever-increasing wind. "The planet went through a period of climate change in which the environment cooled down. Many species failed to survive into the next era."

"There are two areas of suspected weakness in which we intend to focus," Adem said. "In over 10 million years of roaming our earth, this species has left fossilized teeth on the coasts of every continent, except

Antarctica. It would seem that it's unlikely she can survive the cold."

"Secondly, a shark's liver keeps them buoyant. Once removed or injured to the point of dysfunction, they can no longer swim up and down debilitating them," Evelyn relayed.

"If we can capture her, we're hoping to be able to exploit one of these areas?" Adem asked.

"That's the plan." Dru said.

"What, is the plan exactly?" Alex asked.

"The plan is to bait her, capture her, and injure her liver," Evelyn determined.

"Yes, but given her ferocity to this point, we'd be fools to think that this alone will work. So, the next step is to use debilitate her with LN2: Liquid Nitrogen and freeze her to death." TJ explained.

"We have 100 pressurized super-insulated vacuum vessels of the fluid prepared for injection once she's debilitated. We're going to completely suspend her animation." Emmie reported.

"And how are we doing to bait her?" asked Adem taking a long drink from his water bottle.

"Present day sharks can detect vibrations in the water by using a special organ called the lateral line. They also have an amazing sense of smell to communicate through molecules moving across the mucous membrane of the nose. We'll use intense vibrations to lure her into the area and then the chum to bring her into the trap," Evelyn explicated.

Eighteen Hours Later

Weapons were constructed, and the

aquatic resonance speaker transmitted vibratory signals to hail the beast. Adem and Evelyn were perched in an observation tower on watch. Emmie and TJ were in the bunkhouse resting. Alex and Dru were gathering items for a meal in the makeshift mess hall when Adem noticed the seismograph begin to agitate.

"Honey, take a peek at the sat footage. Do you see anything?" After reading the measures, she activated the com system.

"Delta Zulu, Cthulhu Incoming!" she announced on the radio. As the research team assembled and shared the readings, the military troop was collecting, directed by Michaels, as two uniformed people entered the tower. With Alex right behind, Dru was the first to rush into the building. Emmie and TJ came tumbling in just after rubbing sleep from their eyes.

"Dr. Humboldt," the formidable gentleman implored. The husband and wife both turned around. The man was built like a tank and dressed in a sharp uniform dripping in sashes and pendants, which boasted that he was a supreme hero.

"Dr. Evelyn Humboldt," he specified. "I'm told you're the lead researcher on this assignment." Looking at her husband for some type of feedback, Adem had none. He lifted his shoulders, palms up, and shook his head, to which she also shrugged.

"Am I?" she asked. The team had not been briefed or interacted with except when necessary. Politics or procedures were thickly glossed over as their focus was paramount.

"Yes. I'm Commander in Chief Jean Pierre Sibblies overseeing this operation." A striking woman half his size looking twice as harsh in an orderly navy coat and trousers with a single-breasted jacket. The single row of four gold-colored buttons gleamed, decorated with rows of gold sleeve stripes, badges, and service stripes, indicated that she was a force to be reckoned with. The curly-haired, compact commander put out her hand.

"I'm Secretary of the Navy, Elizabeth Torres. I'm overseeing the marine snare. I'm primarily here to assist with damage control. From what's been reported, our likelihood of success is below 10%. What is your assessment?"

"I would say that's accurate," Evelyn admitted. The tension in the air thickened visibly at that report. "And it seems as if we have an incoming heading our way. The troops are readying the trap, and we should have eyes on the target in a few minutes." She pointed to the satellite projections showing a large target beeping traveling ever closer. Silbblies pursed his lips before clenching and releasing his fists to his sides while Torres stretched to stand a bit taller, readying themselves for what was to come. The fear of the great unknown was palpable. At this time, Adem unlocked some orange bins with life jackets and began handing them out. The scientists and military personnel fastened each buckle and adjusted them to fit. Next, Adem strapped a floating pack to his wife and then tethered them together with an elastic cord.

"Wherever you go, I go too." he

whispered to her.

"I love you," she answered without taking her eyes off the scene.

Navy pilots from thirty different areal locations were harnessed with cannon-like harpoon guns readied as the mass approached. It was then that they saw a vast fin breach the water half of a mile away. Evelyn was at the computer, snapping infrared images illustrating that the infinydon's body seemed to have grown since the last footage they saw of her.

"Michaels, she's grown!" She called over the radio. We're going to need all of the canisters of LN2." Michaels didn't even wait to break the connection or ask any follow-up questions before he began barking orders to have the rest of the canisters distributed. The inaudible echo vibrating into the sea was resonating, beckoning to leviathan clearly. Within minutes, the beast covered the distance and swam into the bay into surprisingly shallow water. 50-gallon drums of chum were released to distract her and keep her occupied. As the water began to turn crimson, she began to flail wildly. She couldn't swim well and began pushing back into deeper water frenzied.

"Teams Alpha, Bravo, Charlie: Fire!" Michaels commanded. In almost perfect unison, the harpoon guns were discharged, there was the briefest moment of whirring on cable, and then despite fierce thudding sounds, most of the metal spears fell away from her, unable to penetrate her armored flesh. A few had embedded superficially. Those which had reached an impact point along the border of the scale loculation, were behind the pectoral fin. Noting this, Adem picked up his radio.

"They have to aim for the vulnerable areas between the scales." Knowing that heavy-duty weapons didn't have that type of precision aim on a thrashing moving target, the leader gave the following orders.

"Teams Delta, Echo, Foxtrot: Fire!" Michaels reverberated. She began to flip her body wildly, bending side to side like a salmon slipping from the paws of a grizzly. Waves pounded the struts of the towers, and she knocked out one of the lookouts' peaks with her tail, which held four of the gunmen. They were tossed through the air to their deaths. Propelled from the south tower, one of the cables penetrated behind her dorsal fin. With one twist of her body, the cord snapped and whipped back like an electric lasso cutting down everything in its path. As Dru peered down from the observation deck, being close enough to feel saltwater spray mist her face, her mouth fell open as she stared at a uniformed trunk without a torso that stood momentarily exterminated like a roach before crumpling into a heap in front of her. So many other bodies were strewn. People began yelling but refused to abandon their posts.

Adem noticed the commotion she was causing was swashing the water up and out of the bay; she was stranding herself. Adem thought now was the time.

"Shoot her! Dose her now!" he hollered. Michaels pressed the button on his com.

"Tranc teams one, two, three: Fire!" The soldiers who resembled tiny army men from the lookout point with massive tranquilizer guns began firing, hailing a rainfall of bee-stings against her.

"It will take the darts 15 seconds to inject all of the Nitrogen into her," Adem said into the radio. Seeming to know her time was almost up, she began heaving her body further ashore and snapping her jaws at anything she could reach, rows of teeth gyrating. The power and mass of her body were annihilating everything in her path. The temporary island fort was assembled last week, and its 150 inhabitants were destroyed within minutes.

"If anything is going to happen, it will be immediate." Evelyn continued holding out hope for the safety of the tower. It was then that she saw another prominent figure on the radar imaging. Grabbing the intercom,

"Here comes another one!" she wailed.

"A what?" he screeched. "Hold your fire!" he commanded. They watched their nemesis flip and writhe and fight as the seconds ticked. Suddenly, one canister emptied, dosing her, and they all began to release. An ear-splitting roaring screech sounding not of this world filled the skies. Her back arched. She gave one powerful epic contortion and then began to glaciate. The wind howled as they watched the cryogenic freeze start in her body's middle. She thrashed her head and tail convulsively until she froze into a solid mass, a series of strange popping sounds echoing as she turned into a block of ice. The sound went from ear-piercing screech to an echo as her eyes glazed over, and she froze in an upright position. The team was suddenly looking at an epic prehistoric sculpture which didn't seem possible. A second beast crashed into the bay as they all began to look around.

"Shoot her! Give it everything you've got!" Adem directed over the radio.

"Full throttle!" Michaels commanded, signaling his arms for those without an earpiece. With that, harpoons and guns began blazing at will, some bouncing off and others finding their target. One arrow hit the frozen monstrosity causing her to shatter. The second beast was quickly tethered from six angles, and the group watched as they held her precariously like a cat in the cradle. What now?

"Release the thermonuclear!" Torres commanded over her com.

"Nukes?" Adem yelled. The gigantessa thrashed and keeled, taking out the last two towers and the observation deck, causing men and women to be flung treacherously to their doom.

The observation deck was hit with a lashing fin which caused it to buckle in the center tossing its occupants scattering in every direction. Those who landed on the rocks were dashed and killed. Before Adem knew which direction he was flying, he was underwater, saline filling his lungs. Struggling, he swam toward the shimmering light of the water's surface. He felt something drifting passed him, brushing him ever so gently as fire flashed above them. He saw Evelyn's lifeless body sinking below him, unconscious, contusions bleeding. As the water whipped around him, mirroring the chaos above, she became lodged between two boulders. He pumped his arms and legs with all of his might swimming down. His fingers grabbed the very edge of her life jacket as his last bubble of breath was used up by the exertion. With a frantic jerk, he loosed her from the rocks. Eyes on the light, he saw more explosions detonating above. He swam with all of his might, finally breaching the surface. He was amazed at how far away from the island they were. Shaking her lifeless body, she was suddenly reanimated and began to cough up water.

"There you go, Darling," he encouraged, towing her by the vest. Wet hair plastered to her face, she sputtered, coughing as the air hit her face. He reached up, moving the strangling mask of hair away from her airway. She was burned and battered with oozing lacerations. Surprised that he had fared so well right next to her, he took to examining himself and noticed just as much damage. Thank you, endorphins, he mused, grimacing as the pain began to surface. He paddled, towing her as long as his strength would allow. *To where?* he wondered. *Away*, he rationalized. *But to where?* he asked himself again. In his mind, he recalled the map of the Banda Arc and thought he recalled a freckling of tiny islands surrounding the Arc. Pulling his left arm from under her neck and pulling her up onto his chest, he noticed the flesh sagging off his arm, turning white from lack of blood flow. In his mind, he had a flash of raising his arm up to shelter his face as he turned, tucking his wife under his protective wing, feeling the hair on the back of his head singeing before they were submerged under warm torrential water.

They were far from shore now, where they could see a massive fire burning. He couldn't hear the noises of any people or animals and didn't see any murderous sharks. In truth, he couldn't hear anything at all. Deaf. Well, at least he had his sight.

Dizzy and in deep water, knowing they may be the only moving targets, he decided maybe they should just float. He stopped trying to actively swim and turned on his back. He wriggled downward in the vest, the straps pulling taught under his arms so it would support his head like a pillow. He pulled Evelyn higher up onto his chest. He thought it was a good thing she was pint-sized compared to him. He allowed his feet to float upward so that he was buoyant, using the life jacket on the current like a raft, surprised at how rapidly they were being swept away from the scene. He tied the straps of her life jacket to his to keep her face above water as long he remained afloat on his back.

Alarmed by the lack of salt in the water, he had swallowed. It tasted almost entirely fresh. He worried about who the survivors were and how many more beasts could be lurking. That was the last thought before he lost consciousness reaching for his wife. The two floated away on the freshwater sea, seemingly the only two survivors of the last stand.

CHAPTER THIRTY TWO

BIRD'S EYE VIEW

ON THE COAST of New York City, Delsin and Chris sat on the roof of the four-story library, barefooted, feet dangling in tepid brackish ocean water. The city was quiet, already having been evacuated. Delsin had sent his family back to the rez. They had chosen to spend their last days in ceremonial prayer in hopes of reconnecting with the land. He had to consider that there was a possibility that they may survive being inland. The two vowed to do their best to restore harmony and carry on his message if they were granted their lives. The grid was down in this region. Domestic and wild animals scurried unattended in areas that were still above water. Homo sapien was a rare sight to see. The two men sat together in unabashed companionship.

They spoke, voices echoing, bouncing around the architecture of high-rises eerily devoid of life. They retraced events in their childhoods and shared their hopes, dreams, and achievements in this lifetime. They spoke about what they didn't get to do in this world, regretful.

"I just wish I hadn't wasted time disgracing my ancestors by being so destructive." Delsin expressed. Chris grimaced, commiserating in Del's lamentation. Then he smiled mischievously.

"Have you ever had a girlfriend?" Chris asked him pointedly, one eyebrow up.

"Yes!" Delsin drawled out, laughing. "Wait. Have you?"

"No!" answered Chris, baldly, shaking his head. "And now, I'm going to die a virgin," he confessed, head hanging, loneliness weighing heavily on his shoulders. They looked at each other soberly. Chris was the first to crack a smile, and they both burst into laughter.

"Don't you believe that you're like earning gold coins in heaven or something?" the young man asked of the priest.

"I don't really know," Chris admitted. "Earlier in my life I was certain that it was the right thing to do. I felt for many years that I had a relationship with God. I believed that I was on a divine path. Now, knowing it's all over and seeing all these crazy things that the bible never talked about, I can't say with confidence what is to come." Delsin's head bobbed in understanding as they both stared out over the sparkling water.

"A shark. I thought we had figured that much out." Delsin said idly.

"Well, yes!" Chris said incredulously, shrugging. "A shark is definitely coming, but I mean the afterlife and all. I can't say that I'm not afraid to die. I feel that I've been a good person and I think that I've been honorable even if I've lost my faith. Will I be condemned for that?" He pondered, nodding his head up and down. "Yes. In the church's eyes, most absolutely," he concluded.

"I'm not asking you what your church would say. I'm asking you what you think. I can tell that you are good," Delsin assured him.

"Your god knows that." Delsin put his arm around Chris' shoulder, and they both sat there contemplating life and death. Not only their own but the passing of their whole species and the world as they know it. As they commiserated, the devastation of the world now upon them, they could clearly see ahead.

They spoke of the decimation occurring worldwide: the mudslides, the tornadoes, the volcanic eruptions, the floods, the fires, the diseases, and all the people who had already died. There is a time when all dominant species fall from their thrown to the bottom of the food chain. Man has surpassed that time. Between science, technology, and industry, mankind has become too powerful: godlike. Maybe this entity was sent here by God to kill a god, the human race. It was time, they had agreed. Time to lay down and give thanks for our species' time in this realm. As the two men conveyed their subjective thoughts on the matter, a massive fin broke the surf heading toward them. They continued conversing as she turned and swayed in the swell, weaving back and forth playfully. A peace enveloped them while their inevitable doom approached.

As she neared the coast, the water began to lap excitedly at their calves, agitated by the tremendous water displacement by such a behemoth monster. They sat in solidarity, knowing that their end was near. As she swam, gracefully coming ever closer, Chris reached out for Del. Close now. Her jaw began to open, displaying her unimaginable pink flesh budding row after row of serrated blades. The men could see that she was truly massive.

They witnessed her jaws on rotating sockets that appeared to be coursing back and forth in alternating directions, not unlike a chainsaw. Just as the figment of their visions drew close enough for them to see her nostrils flare, they heard an ear-piercing sound from the sky. Looking up, they saw a projectile materialization from on high. Delsin smiled at the comical whistling sounds as if they were watching a cartoon. It fell as if in slow motion. The two friends closed their eyes and leaned into each other as the bomb fell, made impact, and detonated. Delsin swallowed hard, hearing a roaring wall of water coming toward them. His adam's apple rose slowly but failed to ever descend.

In the time it takes for one electrical impulse to contract and release, stimulating one heartbeat, the blue sky turned white, and their world went silent. As the device impacted the sea, the explosion sucked in millions of gallons of water, creating a massive crater so almighty that it absorbed everything, including the sound. Seconds later, an explosion never witnessed by the human eye began rippling out. Just as quickly, the suction force reversed and, starting with a small ring, the impact undulated out, growing in power with a pulse like a sonic boom. Within a snap, the men were obliterated. Anything within sight and then within driving distance by a day and then even further was blown out of existence.

The swimming entity, all-wise and knowing, with no emotional bond to her exterior shell, was destroyed to all but a molecular level. The matter which had made up her body and mind was dispersed over several miles in an epic geyser comprised of marine water, buildings, boats, cars, the prophets of mother nature, and untold numbers of other forms of life. As quickly as it rose, this fountain of dissolution rained violently back down on the Earth, further destroying everything it touched.

At ground zero, the infinydon, the ocean, and all living beings were zapped into nonexistence. The radius of the impact billowed, blasting everything within the forcefield into oblivion. The two men simply ceased to exist on this plane within the blink of an eye. They left their bodies instantly with the peace of mind that their time was over: Their little flames extinguished. The blast went on for hundreds of miles, killing flora and fauna within its path. Simultaneously, it surged through North America and Central America, the force gradually lessening as it reached the other continents, causing an epic disturbance worldwide.

A massive tidal wave dragged Adem, and Evelyn waterlogged onto an uninhabited tropical island. They lay unconscious, half-drowned and traumatized from the beating of the explosion. The disbanded matter of the colossus began to draw nearer to each other in time, slowly but surely, floating intuitively, magnetically back together. Globules of the prehistoric monstrosities found each other as if through magnetic force. Over months, they formed a harmless embryonic viscous state, mission concluded, they drifted back down into the vast ocean's abyss to sleep until woken by Father Time at the next significant juncture in evolution. The Earth, now abandoned, was left to recover and heal.

CHAPTER THIRTY THREE

ELYSIUM

One Year Later

A LEAN, OLIVE-SKINNED, shaggy-haired Adem came running back toward camp. His eyes ever scanning the lush landscape for his woman, who was last seen in the area collecting fruits and nuts for their evening meal.

"The sun!" he cried out. "I can see the sun on the horizon!" Over the last year, the sky had been obscured by fallout, and dark, angry cloud cover overshadowed the planet; tropical storms had battered them ruthlessly. Vegetation had suffered. The couple worried that their time of plenty in this paradise could come to an end. If the sun failed to emerge, they surmised all the world would eventually perish.

For the first several months, violent storms and tidal waves washed away their homestead, making their work seemly unending. There were earthquakes and hurricane-force winds many days out of the year. Eventually, the storms began to subside.

Wife in tow, he followed the sheen of the celestial body through the thinning mists, running in wildling garb, to the edge of the jungle. They watched in reverence, toes splayed wide in the damp sand, holding each other as they witnessed the beautiful fiery sun setting in the west. They watched the day star until the haze returned, obscuring their night sky view. They stayed, comfortably parked in a cozy nest of a smooth beach tree truck at their backs, the sound of the surf lapping and the calls of the evening jungle dwellers crooning. As far as they could tell, the two seemed to be the only human survivors of the catastrophe they were aware of. There were no signs of life over the radios from their emergency packs, and never were there sightings of seafarers. For the sake of their species, they held hope that there were at least pockets of people who had survived; however, they had no indication of this.

In the beginning, they had been lucky to have a few crude tools in their packs with which to begin again. Soon, pieces of wood and various items had drifted ashore from surrounding islands and the mainland throughout the year. Initially, they had built a shanty quickly torn down by the winds. They reclaimed most of the lumber and rebuilt a more sophisticated shelter than the meager temporary fort. This new home they called the ramada because it had an actual roof attached to posts and beams with an adjoined porch that comfortably sheltered them. Fortuitously, they were surrounded by the prolific gardens of the tropics with healthy animals and plants to support them. There was no need for farming. They set a few traps for animals when they needed protein but were learning to gain essential nutrients from the nuts and beans that grew around them. When they had the time, they would scavenge eggs.

As the days passed, they became less concerned about being rescued and relaxed into the immense peace of living in harmony with the animals. As the weather became less tempestuous, Adem chose to expand the domicile. Evelyn suggested that they build upward, not out, to minimize their footprint. With barrels, they collected freshwater. They soon relaxed into a cycle of falling asleep with the sun's setting and waking with the dawn. Any waste they created was compostable; they truly lived as one with the world.

As days melded into weeks, seasons ripened and waned. After a time, the sun shown more often. Flowers bloomed, clean, crisp rains fell, floodwaters receded, and the sea life began to reinvigorate. The lovers found comfort in this strange land as the earth regenerated herself. They grew strong and supple, learning the ways of this new world, their shelter protecting them from the jagged edges of the wild.

The world's apocalyptic injuries matured from festering wounds into tight, punishing scabs under which she knitted herself back together. These crustations eventually softened and, with healing forgiveness and fell away. Her lesions grew from angry, swollen abrasions to shiny taut seams, which were honored interpreters of her tale. They sang the epic of a victorious battle after which Mother Earth flourished. In this calm, the island became a beautiful tranquil place, a haven, and their home became a comfortable place.

Following the exemplar of the land, the animals flourished. The shelter of the humans progressed into living quarters that were half indoor and half outdoor. They had collapsible doors that could be opened and closed, but they remained propped open these days even throughout most nights. Their refined shelter encompassed a modest living area as they prospered. They built a place for preparing food, a cozy loft for sleeping that was safe from large animals even though only a few rodent-sized blurs were ever glimpsed. Adem even constructed an impressive crow's nest from which they could survey the ocean to spot incoming storms.

The scientists developed an intimate knowledge of the land and the sea. From the taste, they observed that the water was becoming increasingly saline once again and was pleased to see the marine life recovering. They built crude traps in the bay and finally began catching fish. It was weeks before they caught the first small insignificant snack, but by spring's end, their treasury was bursting. On a daily basis, they were consuming nourishing plant life using cut-and-come-again methods in which they took a portion of edible parts of the plant but left a majority of the plant and root system intact so that it could continue to grow to be harvested multiple times.

Life became peaceful, the land growing fruitful. Joyously, their quality of life improved. Once no longer fighting for survival, the two spent increasing energy exploring the jungle together, marveling at the miracle of life and studying the multitude of wildlife. They began to learn about all their neighbors. The two became aware of leopards, throngs of birds, wild dog or red wolf species, crocodilians, pythons, some large cats, and giant lizard monitors. The felines stayed far away, but they had seen glimpses of them when foraging deep in the forest.

A few sun-dappled pythons had slithered harmlessly through their camp and spotted others in the trees. The couple debated whether or not the animals were becoming less wary of them or if they were simply getting better at spotting them. They finally agreed that it was likely a combination of the two.

Much to Evelyn's delight, there was a specific wolf who had begun lurking around their base. Her pack had been spotted living up near the cliffs. A singular female had taken an interest in the people, which Evie named Kailani after the sea and the sky. In the springtime, the lady wolf grew distant as she raised a litter of pups. When she came back around, one little adventurer grew increasingly bold. After weeks of taunting, he took a bite of fish offered out of Evelyn's hand. He nabbed the bite and retreated in terror. Evelyn howled with laughter. After the encounter, he stayed away for a week. Soon enough, they began spotting him again, watching them from afar and closer thereafter.

By late spring, he visited them daily, sitting and observing these strange two-legged primates. They would toss him scraps and speak to him in gentle tones. One day, he found himself shyly begging for snacks. Thus began Adem's daily ritual of early morning fishing and leaving one out just for him. During high summer, the couple woke to find that he had spent the night in their camp. That night she named him Nyx, which means night, and said he was now her dog. He was red with a black muzzle and paws.

Two species of birds took up residence within their fort and began cleaning up the crumbs and even allowing hand-feeding at times. There was a large flock of flame-breasted sunbirds. Although this species seemed to be primarily nectarivorous, they seemed interested in the activities of these new bipedal animals. They appreciated the large ambrosial blooms growing in and around their habitat due to the water stored within. These songbirds called and sang to introduce the dawning day. As lovely as they were, Evie enjoyed the gentle music and colorful showing of a small, plump species of a sparrow with a hefty bill, white cheeks, orange feet, and tangerine bellies. What a darling alarm clock they made.

One of Adem's favorites were the Sunda sambar deer. They were large, dark, long-haired, antlered deer with charming wide-set ears and glistening child-like eyes. They lived in small herds and were, at first, very shy. The newcomers were surprised when a herd wandered into their camp early one morning, and an antlered stag let out an alarming honk when startled by them when they emerged into the clearing. They were like quiet sleeper agents living their secret lives in the wilderness until their breeding season came along. Impressively musty stags began combatting hind-legged while making all manner of unearthly noises: screams and other terrifying cacophonies of agitation. The does would also stomp or even rear and hit other animals with their heads upon threat. Shortly after one of these fierce tournaments, Evelyn saw one of the does with a bright red bald patch on her chest that, from a distance, was perceived as an injury. Soon, she saw other females with the same marking and began to suspect disease. Later, she noticed the does with the ruddy markings had calves afoot and were nursing young.

When tiny wobbly-legged toddlers appeared in the fawning season, Evelyn started feeling the exhilaration of renewal mixed mildly with a pang of sadness that they would never be blessed with offspring. Evelyn was especially delighted to see one mother doe with twins. She then realized she hadn't experienced her menses in several weeks? How many weeks, she queried. She had really lost track time of time. She put on hand up to her flat belly in bewilderment.

The days grew longer, and the two became more comfortable with the island as their home. The island was thriving; the crisis abated. The sky continued to clear, seeds germinated, and the jungle blossomed and grew more heavily ripe with life rebounding. Giant robust fruits hung and fell from trees. Reptiles, wildfowl, and mammals all share in the bounty.

Time marched on. Husband and wife developed an evening ritual following supper of ambling down the path to the shore and watching the sunset. They marveled at the chromatic pastel kaleidoscopic dramatically painting artwork in the sky, a perfect conclusion to each sunny day. They listened, breathing deeply, as the world embraced the night's calm, an orchestra of invertebrate and amphibian nocturnals waking in time to lull the diurnal creatures to sleep.

One of these evenings, in the crux of her husband's lap, without warning, Evelyn felt a quickening in her belly, a barely perceptible flurry. Her lips quirked at the gentle foreign sensation. Her mate, who knew her better than she knew herself, smiled as he reached over and put his rough hand across her exposed midriff.

"I think I'm-,"

"Of course, you are." he responded matter-of-factly.

"How do you know?" she asked, turning.

"You haven't bled in too long, which has

been nice. You were making a dreadful mess." She pushed him back into the sand, smiling. "- and we've had so much time for recreation the last few months." He drawled, eyebrows raised.

"Yes, but I've lost weight. I assumed I stopped ovulating because of the duress coupled with being so dangerously thin." she reasoned.

Reaching for her, he pointed out, "Stress? You're more fit, healthy, and relaxed than you've been in your whole life. You are lean but your muscled not underweight. Your infertility before was probably stress-related," he conjectured. "I've thought a lot about what I want, a boy or a girl, and decided that I don't care. I just want a small person that's made from us with whom we can share our life." Her eyes widened with realization and adoration at how much time he'd spent considering this possibility.

"You do?" she urged, nuzzling her cheek into his chest, feeling so securely loved.

"I do." he said as he gave her hip a squeeze kissing the side of her head. "Maybe we should follow Kailani's example and have a whole litter of them." He mused quietly as the warm darkness fell, gently blanketing them.

"Do you think, we are the only lucky ones,." she asked, heartache thick in her voice. "What did we do to deserve another chance while everyone else was lost?"

"It wasn't up to us. So, don't feel guilty. Be glad. We're here. We're alive against all odds and we're thriving. That's nature. That's life." He responded simply

"You really are a scientist to the core." she reveled. He shrugged, not arguing her point. "Since we are just animals. How many generations of our species do you think have come before us?" she asked him.

"Mmm... I figure less than 500?" he guessed.

"And now, here comes one more!" he proclaimed nearly growling.

"Yes, my beast. We are making at least one more." Beaming with the possibilities of what the future may hold, standing solitary in time, Adem and Eve walked back home hand-in-hand through their beautiful garden of redemption. The three were on a path to rebuild humanity, a gentler, wiser race of humankind in harmony with earth once again.

ABOUT THE AUTHOR

Marita Christine Lorbiecke is an American author who was raised in the company of books and fascinating intellects, especially her mother, who did not live to see her children into adulthood due to a terrible tragedy. Her mother was a lover of books, a philanthropist, and somewhat of an animal whisperer, which Marita inherited through example. Growing up in nature, she became enamored with wildlife of all kinds and grew up marrying and having children within a menagerie of exotic animals. To this day, Marita and her husband live on a farm and own a private zoo that features hundreds of beautiful birds, giant tortoises and lizards, massive snakes, marsupials, and miniature livestock. She is a veteran educator in public schools as well as online. Marita attended college in New Mexico, earning several degrees, accolading a Master's degree. She works as a professional belly dancer, model, and snake wrangler in her spare time. She is a true romantic and is happy to be living out the ultimate dream life with her husband, the real Dr. Humbolt, John D Lorbiecke.

EPIGRAPH

One Hundred Love Sonnets: XVII
BY PABLO NERUDA
TRANSLATED BY MARK EISNER

I don't love you as if you were a rose of salt, topaz,
or arrow of carnations that propagate fire:
I love you as one loves certain obscure things,
secretly, between the shadow and the soul.

I love you as the plant that doesn't bloom but carries
the light of those flowers, hidden, within itself,
and thanks to your love the tight aroma that arose
from the earth lives dimly in my body.

I love you without knowing how, or when, or from where,
I love you directly without problems or pride:
I love you like this because I don't know any other way to love,
except in this form in which I am not nor are you,
so close that your hand upon my chest is mine,
so close that your eyes close with my dreams.

Pablo Neruda, "One Hundred Love Sonnets: XVII" from The Essential Neruda: Selected Poems, edited by Mark Eisner. Copyright © 2004 City Lights Books.
Source: The Essential Neruda: Selected Poems (City Lights Books, 2004)

Made in the USA
Coppell, TX
30 June 2022